My Guardian Angel

My Guardian Angel

LANNY SAUMER

iUniverse

My Guardian Angel

iUniverse books may be ordered through booksellers or by contacting:

iUniverse
1663 Liberty Drive
Bloomington, IN 47403
www.iuniverse.com
844-349-9409

ISBN: 978-1-4401-6923-6 (sc)
ISBN: 978-1-4401-6924-3 (hc)

Print information available on the last page.

iUniverse rev. date: 07/11/2022

Dedication

I dedicate this book to my mother and to my wonderful brother and sisters and of course to my father, who kept his vow to mother and turned out to be a gracious grandfather to 15 grandchildren and died at the age of 82; God bless his soul. I also dedicate this book to my best friend and wife, Karen, and my amazing sons Brandon, Shane, and Travis and my beloved daughter, Stacia, as well as my grandchildren. I also want to thank all the countless friends and family who have been a part of my life through thick and thin. Many of you are mentioned in this book and you all mean the world to me. God has truly blessed me!

Preface

January 27th, 1949, was pure hell for my father. He had spent the evening before at his wife's hospital bedside celebrating the birth of their second son on the 21st and his own fortieth birthday on the 26th. Mom had spent six days in the hospital recovering from complications due to my delivery. From what I've been told, she was not to have any more children after my youngest sister was born four years earlier. Mom had been given the "OK" to go home on the 27th. There would be plenty of help at home with four other children: sixteen year old Betty, fourteen year old Jill, seven year old Kenneth, and four year old Carol. For Herb and Ruth Saumer and baby Lanny, life was good.

Dad finished shaving and had a quick bite of breakfast. The kids were all excited. Dad was going to the hospital to bring Mom and baby brother home today. Dad gave everyone their usual morning hug and kiss. He got into his forty -six Ford Coupe and drove off for the hospital. As he drove along, he couldn't help but think about how great a day his birthday had been. All his prayers had been answered. His wife had recovered from her complications and they were bringing home a healthy baby boy. He stopped at the local florist and picked up some flowers for Mom.

The tension in the hospital was so thick you could cut it with a knife. Everyone was looking at Dad with faces white as ghosts. Everything was so quiet. As Dad approached Mom's room, he was met by her doctor. Within the last hour before Dad arrived at the hospital, a blood clot had caused Mom to have a massive heart attack. Dad's beloved Ruth was gone! From that moment on, life would never be the same for Herb Saumer and his five children.

As for me, I never got to know my mother other than through stories and pictures. I know she was a beautiful woman because I have a picture of her standing by a tree, and she looks just like my sister Carol. I know she was musically talented, as she sang in the church choir and wrote and published a song called "Under the Spell of The Moon". I know that Dad loved her dearly and vowed to her that he would always keep the family together; a vow that would prove to be difficult for Dad to keep. I believe that from the moment Mom died, God gave her the assignment to be My Guardian Angel. Boy, have I needed her!

The ten years that followed our mother's death would prove to be a living hell on earth for the Saumer family. Dad took Mom's death very hard, and as so many mourning people do, took to the bottle. He would drink away his pay checks. We lost home after home because he wouldn't pay the rent, and the homes we did live in weren't fit to live in. For the first three years of my life, I lived with my Aunt and Uncle along with their two daughters, both older than me. My sister, Carol, lived with another set of cousins in the cities. Brother, Ken, stayed with our Grandma and Grandpa Gamm. Betty and Jill pretty much took care of themselves and Dad as much as they could. The break-up of the family made Dad even more depressed, so he drank even more. Dad wanted the family back together to keep his vow to Mom.

When my aunt gave birth to a son, I was three years old. Dad saw an opportunity to reunite the family. He figured I was out of diapers and potty trained, walking and talking, and eating regular food. Therefore, I wouldn't be as much work for the rest of the kids. Carol was seven and would be in all day school along with Ken, who was ten. Betty had graduated from High School and Jill had dropped out of school, so they could look after me. It seemed like it should all work out fine. Who knew what a little devil had been born into this world on January 21st, 1949.

Each chapter of this book is a short story about a life altering event that I believe God and My Guardian Angel Mother has seen me through. In some cases, one might say it is also a book of confessions. Although each story is based on a true event, some of which took place over forty and fifty years ago, I have had to use writer's privilege and add a little color here and there.

Contents

PART ONE
SMITH ADDITION

Chapter One
"KIDS SAY AND DO THE DARNDEST THINGS"

*T*o say that I presented a problem or two for the family during my developmental years would be putting it mildly. I was as stubborn as a mule, mischievous as a raccoon, smart as a fox, and independent and strong as a grizzly; a force to be reckoned with. My first memory of my childhood is a walk I took to the city swimming pool about five blocks from our home in Montevideo, Minnesota. I remember sneaking in and going swimming in the kiddy pool. I remember seeing the army trucks parked by the National Guard Armory next to the pool. It was also the summer we moved across town down to Smith Addition, so I must have been only three or four years old. I was gone for a long time, and when I returned, I remember everyone being so upset. That was the first of many explorations, trials, and tribulations that God and My Guardian Angel have seen me through in sixty years.

Smith Addition was the poor side of town in Montevideo, Minnesota, which is tucked away in the Chippewa River valley. Monte hasn't changed a lot since I left there in 1967. The population has remained somewhat stagnant at around five thousand. It remains primarily a farming community. Most of the town is "up on the hill", where all the schools, today's modern retail stores, motels, and fast food restaurants are. Despite being the poor side of town, Smith Addition had several unique and adventurous qualities for a young boy growing up in the 1950s.

To enter Smith Addition, you had to cross over the Chippewa River, which flows down from the North and empties into the Minnesota River at the South end of town. Just before crossing the bridge over the Chippewa, the road went through a set of parks, Smith Park on the left and Lagoon Park on the right. As you entered Smith Addition, you first came across a small business and industrial area. It had a corner grocery store. Across the street from the grocery store was a farm implement dealer, and next to that was a Studebaker car dealer, and across the highway from that was a lumber yard. About four blocks to the North end of the addition was a construction company, with several old warehouse buildings and lots of machinery. Beyond the construction company was the forest, with the Chippewa River running through it. To the West were the railroad, the stock yard, and Swifts, where my father worked making butter. Our home, at 604 Kingman Street, and each of these locations in Smith Addition provided me with a world of fantasy, adventure, and juvenile crime during the eight years we lived there.

I remember moving into the basement house in Smith Addition. You had to walk down a flight of stairs to enter the house. I remember falling down those steps on more than one occasion. When you entered the house through a door at the bottom of the stairs, you were met by a checkered floor in the kitchen. The home was heated by a parlor stove in the living room next to the kitchen. There were two bedrooms and a small bathroom with a shower. Dad and Ken shared one bedroom and Carol and I shared the other. The walls of the house were cinder block with small windows at the top, through which only a small child could crawl in or out. The house was on a beautiful corner lot almost smack dab in the middle of Smith Addition. The lot had a few trees on it and a big empty lot with a small hill next to it; it was actually a pretty neat place to live. One of the most memorable routine events of our time in Smith addition, was when Grandpa Harry Saumer would come on Sunday and play Cribbage with Dad. To this day I love playing Cribbage.

Dad would work all day and then stop at the bar and drink before coming home. Ken and Carol were always off doing their things with their friends. I would be with my own friends; everyone was older than me. Being the youngest in the neighborhood had advantages and disadvantages. Most everyone was pretty nice to me. I don't remember anyone ever being cruel to me just to be cruel. I did get into a spat or two with a couple of my friends. For the most part everyone just left me alone. It was all the alone time that filled my world with adventure and trouble in Smith Addition.

To this day, I'm not sure what strings Dad had to pull to keep me out of reform school when I was seven years old and in second grade. Every day I would stop in at Art's Grocery store and get some kind of snack. Dad had a charge account there, so it was easy to get the snack and charge it. Most of the time, I think Art just pretended to put it on the account. For the most part, Art was a good man; he was a little crude but a good man. He always liked to flirt with the young girls and women. Art only closed his store on Sunday evenings. One Sunday, I saw Art leave the store and go into his home next door. I noticed that he had left one of the doors to the store open. I knew there was a pop machine just inside the door, so I entered the store and got a pop from the machine. Since I was in the store, I figured I might as well take a look around. I wandered around for a few minutes looking at stuff on the shelves. All of a sudden the lights came on, and I heard footsteps in the store. I quickly and very quietly moved to the rear of the store and hid behind some aisle shelving. There was no reason for Art to know I was there. If I waited long enough, he would just leave, and I would be fine and could get away without anyone knowing I had been there. It seemed like Art was there forever. He always whistled while he worked and would sing a tune or two. I could hear him doing things behind the counter— shuffling papers, opening and closing the cash register. I felt the tension, as the fear of getting caught raged through my body. Finally, the lights went out and I heard the door close.

I waited to make sure Art wasn't coming back. The store was mostly dark, except for light shining from the corner street light through the window. As I walked past the counter, I noticed that the cash register was open. I went around to the back of the counter. There it was, I saw more money than I had ever seen. I had no idea as to how much it really was. I took a paper sack from under the counter and put all the money in it. I slid out the door, locked and closed it behind me as I left. To this day, I don't know why I did what I did.

When I got home, Dad's car was in front of the house. I couldn't go into the house with the sack of money. I was in enough trouble already for coming home late, which meant I would get a couple of licks with his belt. I decided to hide the money in a tin can and put it in the rain gutter in the back of the house.

Sure enough, as usual, Dad yelled, "Where the hell have you been?"

Then followed a cuff behind the head, he ramrodded me to the bedroom for a couple of swipes with the belt, and then he sent me to bed without supper. I laid there thinking about what I had done; how it felt, how I had out-foxed Art, how I had gotten away without being caught. I didn't think about the fact that I had just committed a crime; I probably didn't know what a crime was.

The true innocence and stupidity of a seven year old came through the next day. It was Monday and time to go back to school. Before going to get on the school bus, I went and got the tin cup of money. I folded all the money, put it in my pockets, and headed off to catch the school bus. The bus stop was in front of Art's store. When I came through the alley, I saw a police car in front of the store. Two officers were checking the door and walking around looking at the store windows. I got in line to board the bus and watched, as the officers and Art checked everything. The other kids were wondering what all the fuss was about. I wasn't going to let them know I knew.

Growing up we would watch a television show called "Art Linkletter's House Party". A segment of that show was about how "kids say and do the darndest things". Well, that afternoon I did the darndest thing. During lunch recess, I thought I would make some new friends. I started passing out some of my newly acquired money to kids on the playground. I told them that my grandfather had passed away and left me all this money.

When recess was over, I was called to the office. One of the students had told our teacher that I was giving away money on the playground. The principal and teacher asked over and over where I had gotten the money. I stuck to my story. The rest of that day at school was over for me; Dad came and took me home. I got quite a beating when we got there!

Later that evening, I saw Dad talking to Art in front of our house. I don't remember how much money I had stolen, but I know Dad made some kind of an arrangement with Art to keep me from going to juvenile court and reform school. I don't think Dad ever told Ken and Carol about what I had done. At the time I didn't appreciate it too much. I was in pain and hated my father for beating me all the time.

Chapter Two
FOREST ADVENTURES

*T*he Chippewa Forest was a world full of mystery, adventure, and danger. To get to the forest, we had to go through Peterson Brothers Construction equipment and storage yard. Sometimes, we would get side tracked and end up playing on some of the construction equipment or play cops and robbers around the buildings. Once we got through the storage yard, it was easy to see where to get into the forest. Over the years, kids had made a well defined path winding through the woods. A creek split the forest into two distinct parts. The point of entry was distinctly broadleaf trees, mostly elm, maple, box-elder, river willow, and a few oak. When we crossed over the creek, we entered a white pine forest to the left of the trail and a broadleaf forest to the right. On the far side of the forest was the Chippewa River.

Our favorite area was the pine forest. With a little non-voluntary help from Peterson Brothers with materials, we made some very elaborate forts. We created our own little village of four or five huts. Just about every kid in Smith addition was involved with the forest village, so nobody ever did any big damage to the huts; they seemed to last forever and helped us keep dry in the summer and warm in the winter.

My Guardian Angel had to perform some special works the summer and winter I was eight years old. That summer, two of my friends and I decided to spend the day playing in the woods. We had finished some work on the forts and were cleaning up the area when I heard Leon yelling to Wayne and me from the top of a twenty foot pine tree.

"Hey, watch this!" he yelled.

We looked up and saw Leon swaying the top of the tree back and forth until he could almost touch the top of another tree. Suddenly, he went flying through the air from the top of one tree to the top of the other tree like a monkey in the Amazon Rain Forest.

"Man, was that neat!" he shouted down to us, "You've got to climb a tree and do this!"

Leon began swaying back and forth again and leaped from one tree to another; it looked so easy and so fun. With little hesitation, Wayne and I each scampered up to the top of a tree. Leon was right; the rush from playing monkey was incredible. Everything about it made a lasting impression— the smell of the pine trees, the pine sap on your fingers, the pine needles in your face as you climbed the tree, the feeling of swaying back and forth on the tree top, the anticipation of letting go at just the right moment to fly over to the next tree, the freedom of flight, and the panic of finding a branch to grab hold of and hang onto for dear life. The three of us played monkey for quite some time that afternoon.

After making several jumps from tree to tree, the inevitable happened. I had the tree swaying pretty good. I had my eye on the branch I wanted to grab on the other tree. I was ready to fly! Everything went according to plan, except for one thing. I flew through the air and reached for the branch; there it was. I had timed it perfectly. The branch hit my chest, as I wrapped my arms around it. Then I heard it, a loud crack like a tree timbering over. The branch snapped away from the trunk of the tree, and I was heading to the ground 20 feet below. Everything happened so fast. It's amazing how fast you can think when life threatening things happen to you. I kept reaching for branches to grab hold of but couldn't hold on. I hit my head on one branch only to ricochet and hit my back on another one. Down and down I went; I hadn't felt the worst of it yet. Upon impacting the ground, I landed on my tail-bone and got the wind knocked out of me. I panicked and gasped for breath.

When I finally got my breath, I yelled, "I broke my butt!"

The pain was excruciating; running all the way up my back. I unbelievably ran around yelling about how I had broken my butt. Leon and Wayne climbed down from their trees to come to my aid.

"Jump into the river!" Leon shouted. "The cold water will make the pain go away," he explained.

They didn't have to say another word. I ran to the river and jumped in. The swift moving summer water of the Chippewa River wasn't cold but it was cool. I soaked in the water, as my feet sank into the mucky bottom, but I didn't care, it felt so good!

Who knows what kind of injuries I had sustained that day in the forest. I might have had a concussion or a broken back; I wasn't going to say anything to anybody. Dad would have whipped me and grounded me if he had found out, and there would have been medical bills to pay. Through all the pain, I just kept quiet and never said anything to anyone. My Guardian Angel had taken care of me!

The following winter, a second incident took place on the Chippewa River near our little forest village. The Montevideo Public Ice Skating Rink was on the Chippewa River just up stream from the dam. It was common practice for kids to skate up river from the skating rink a couple of miles, usually to the water treatment plant. The river wound around, and it made for quite an adventure. We always had to be on the look-out for open water where the current was too strong for the water to freeze.

One Saturday afternoon, my sister Carol was going to go skating upstream with some friends. Wayne and Gloria lived across the street from us, so we were always close friends. Carol and Gloria were the same age. Wayne was a couple of years older than me. Leon lived a couple of blocks down the street and was the same age as Wayne. Of course being the little pest that I could be, I insisted on tagging along. After all, I could skate better that any of them. What trouble could I cause? Carol agreed to let me go with them.

We started out on our skating adventure upstream. After skating a few hundred yards, we came across an open spot in the ice where we tested to see how much the river had frozen. The more the river had frozen, then the smaller the hole would be. The cold winter had produced fewer open spots. The ice was thick and safe; we could go farther upstream than usual. We proceeded to head upstream to the water plant. I had gone upstream beyond the water plant by walking the bank in the summer before, but I had never gone any farther than the water plant on ice. We all agreed that since the ice was so thick it would be okay to go a little farther upstream to our little forest village. As we approached the village, we could see that there was open water in front of the clearing on the village bank.

Carol cautioned everyone, "Stay close to the bank and away from the open water."

When we finally got to the village, Leon started a fire. The rest of us gathered wood. We sat around the blazing fire and got warm. The smell and crackle of the fire, along with the warmth of the sun, should have made for quite a pleasant rest before our trip back to the rink. However, remember "kids say and do the darndest things".

My curiosity had gotten the best of me. I just had to find out how thick that ice was by the open water in front of the village. Without saying anything to anyone, I got up and slowly skated out to the open water. I could see the water flowing swiftly in the open area. How close could I get to see the water better? Not very far!

"Crash!" went the ice.

I heard the ice crack and give way. Before I could do anything, I was in the ice cold water. The current was so swift it pulled me under the ice, and I popped up again a few feet downstream. I was able to grab hold of the edge of the ice. I tried to get out, but the edges of the ice just kept breaking off.

"Help! Help! " I yelled over and over again.

Carol heard my cry for help and came to the riverbank and saw me fighting for my life. She started screaming for help and running out to rescue me. I just hung on for dear life!

"Stop running Carol or you'll end up in the river with Lanny!" yelled Wayne.

"What can we do?" exclaimed Carol "We have to save him!"

Leon was a pretty bright ten year old boy. He slowly got on his knees on the ice about ten feet from where I was clinging to the edge of the ice. He went to his belly and had Wayne sit on the ice and grab him by the ankles with Gloria and Carol pulling back on Wayne. They slowly inched their way out to me. Leon grabbed my wrists and pulled me out of the ice cold water, while Wayne, Gloria, and Carol pulled Leon back. We all slid to the shoreline together.

We got the fire roaring again, so I could dry out before we headed back to the rink. We had left our shoes back at the skating rink warming house so we had to return to there before going to the warmth and safety of home. Carol kept our little adventure a secret throughout the years knowing how Dad would react. That night, as My Guardian Angel tucked me in for the night, our little basement house in Smith Addition seemed to be the best place on earth.

Chapter Three

MACARONI AND CHEESE

*M*uch like the Chippewa Forest, the stock-yard and railroad provided kids with quite a fantasy world. It was a rather lengthy trek to the stock- yard. We had to walk, about a mile uphill along the highway west of town, out to where Dad worked at Swifts. I usually took a short cut across the field to make sure Dad didn't see me. Once we got to Swifts, we walked the railroad tracks another mile to the abandoned stock- yard.

The stock-yard was a great place to play cowboys. There were all kinds of obstacles to hide behind—pens, ramps, water troughs, and a small building. To make our fantasy a little more real, we would take our BB guns with us. I remember the "Smack" of a BB hitting wood. I don't recall anyone ever getting seriously hurt from being shot with a BB; maybe a little sting now and then. We would play for hours and then make the long trek back home.

"Hey Lanny, isn't that your dad?" asked Punky.

"Oh shit!" I replied, as I ducked behind a box car. "If he sees me, I'm dead!"

We all hid behind the box car and watched Dad walk from Gundy's Lunch back up the hill to the Swifts plant. It was early afternoon and he had made his daily trip down to the diner for lunch. As we watched my dad, we could see the labor of his work all over his clothes.

"What does your dad do here?" Punky questioned.

"He makes butter," I answered.

"You mean like the kind we get in stores?" Punky responded.

"Sort of, I guess," I replied. "He makes it into big balls; after it cools, they cut it into the small blocks you buy in the stores."

Punky surprised me with, "That's pretty neat. The next time I put butter on my toast, I'll think of your dad."

I had never thought about my dad's job being pretty neat. I only knew that he didn't like his job and that it kept him away from home all the time. When Dad finally disappeared into the plant, we continued our journey back home. As we passed in front of Gundy's Lunch, Punky came up with some more questions.

"Have you ever been inside Gundy's?" he asked me.

"Sure, lots of times," I said, with a slight bit of cockiness. "Dad sends me out here to get him cigarettes."

"Yeah, right, how are you able to get cigarettes? You're just a kid!" Punky said with an air of doubt.

"He writes a note for me to give to them and they give me the cigarettes," I explained.

Punky argued with me all the way home about my dad giving me notes to get him cigarettes. When we got home, Punky came up with this big test to see if I was telling the truth.

"Prove to us that you can get cigarettes at Gundy's!"

"How can I prove that?" I asked.

Punky proceeded to outline his plan, "We'll write a note for you to get cigarettes for your dad. You go into Gundy's and get them. If you do it all the time, you shouldn't have any problem."

I didn't want to do it. I knew we were headed for trouble.

"How will we pay for them?" I asked, hoping to put an end to the idea.

"I've got some money at home, come over tomorrow and we'll get it, write the note, and go back to Gundy's."

Punky had all the answers. If I didn't go along with his idea, he would figure me to be a liar. I wasn't lying and I would prove it to him.

"All right, go ahead and write the stupid note! I'll show you!"

The next morning, we went to Punky's house to write the note and get the money. Punky lived in one of the nicer homes in Smith Addition about two blocks away from us. His older brother, Bob, was a good friend of my brother. We had played basketball in their driveway a couple of times, but I had never been in their home before. I remember being quite envious of the carpeted rooms with all the nice furniture. Punky even had a room of his own. Both of Punky's parents worked so there wasn't anyone home at the time.

"I'm hungry! Do you want some milk and cookies?" Punky asked, as he opened the cookie jar on the kitchen counter.

"Sure!" I said without hesitation. I had never seen a cookie jar so full of cookies.

As we ate cookies and drank our milk, Punky started to write the note.

"What does your dad write on the note?" he asked.

"Because I am ill, please allow my son, Lanny, to purchase one pack of Lucky Strike Cigarettes."

Punky started writing the note, then stopped and asked, "How do you spell cigarettes?"

We had the note, and we had the money. We were set to put our plan in action. As we approached Gundy's, I could feel the tension building inside me. I had gotten cigarettes for Dad like this a dozen times before; why was I so scared? Punky hid around the back corner of the diner, as I went inside. I stood at the end of the counter and waited for Gundy.

"Hey there Mr. Saumer, what can I do for you today?" Gundy knew I liked it when he called me Mr. Saumer.

"Hi, Gundy, my dad sent me with this note," I replied, as I handed him the note.

Gundy gave me a questioning look as he read the note. I knew something was wrong. We had been caught; I was as good as dead! He then turned around, went to the cigarette shelf, and brought me the pack of cigarettes.

"Tell your dad I hope he's feeling better soon." He smiled and handed me the cigarettes.

"WOW!" Punky quietly exclaimed, as I showed him the pack of Lucky Strikes. "You really can get cigarettes with a note from your dad."

I was relieved; the note had worked, and I had proven that I wasn't a liar.

As if we hadn't had enough excitement for the day, Punky blurted out his next great idea, "Let's go to the 'culvert' and smoke some."

The "culvert" was a huge railroad culvert about a block away from Gundy's. It was big enough for a kid to stand up, so we often used it as a fort. It was about mid-afternoon, so there was plenty of time to go there for a couple of smokes and get home for supper. I didn't want to miss out on supper that night because Dad had promised to make one of my favorites, macaroni and cheese.

Ken and Carol were already home when I walked in the door. Carol was setting the table, and I could smell the macaroni and cheese.

"Much later and you would have been going to bed without supper young man," Dad grumbled from in front of the cooking stove.

He made the best macaroni and cheese ever, using fresh cheese that he would bring home from Swifts. As I was just about finished with my second helping, Dad stood up from the table and without saying a word unbuckled his belt and started pulling it through his pants loops. This familiar action meant only one thing; I was in big trouble!

Dad placed his belt on the table and sat back down. You could see the panic on Ken's and Carol's faces. They too knew dad was upset about something. Dad then reached into his shirt pocket and took out his pack of Lucky Strike cigarettes and placed them on the table next to his belt. I could see tucked inside the clear plastic wrapper of the cigarette package was a piece of paper.

Dad looked at me with a sternness that I had never seen before. "So young man, I hear you like to smoke!"

"No, Sir!" I lied.

"Then tell me what this is all about!" he said, as he pulled the note out from the cigarette package.

"I don't know," I lied again.

"You don't know?" Dad shouted, as he pounded his fist on the table.

"This stunt wasn't too bright!" Dad exclaimed. "Didn't you think I would find out about this note? I eat lunch at Gundy's every day. He knew this note wasn't from me. He could tell from other notes that my writing doesn't look like this one. When I ate lunch there today he gave me this note and told me you had been in this morning with it—but you don't know anything about it!"

Meanwhile, Ken and Carol knew the scene was going to get ugly. I had committed the trifecta of deceit; I had forged a note from Dad, I had smoked, and now I was lying. They asked if they could be excused.

Dad told them, "Sit there! I want you to see this."

As he put another helping of macaroni and cheese on my plate, he explained, "I am going to give you a choice. You can eat macaroni and cheese and smoke cigarettes until you have to puke, or you can get the beating of your life."

Anything was better than the belt!

I continued to smoke for several years. To this day, I don't understand why one of my favorite meals is still "Macaroni and Cheese".

Chapter Four

BROKEN WINDOW CAPER

Across from Art's grocery store was the Allis Chalmers Farm Implement dealership and the Studebaker Garage. Both places provided me with yet another fantasy world. I would spend hours by myself playing on the farm equipment and racing the abandoned cars. I especially liked climbing up into the combines and pretending to be a farmer like my brother-in-law, Donny.

One day, while I was playing on one of the combines, I noticed that a window was broken in the back of the implement building. Directly below the window was a huge tractor tire leaning up against the building. I figured I could climb that tire to look in the window to see what was inside the building; So, I did. It was actually quite easy for a ten year old boy. The big treads of the tractor tire served as a ladder to the window. I was small enough not to cause the tire to move. Once I got to the top of the tire, I could see clearly into the building. The window was at the end of a loft walk-way for supplies. I could easily climb through the window and get onto the walk-way, go down the steps at the far end and have access to the entire building.

Even though I had been playing on their equipment for years, I had never been inside the implement building before. I got down from the tire, went around to the front of the building and went in through the front door. I walked around pretending to be looking at things; I had no clue as to what all I was looking at. I noticed where the door from the rear work area was, where the pop machines were, and where the cash register was. I decided that I would come back that night, enter through the window and see what I could take.

After supper, I asked Dad if I could go play basketball. He consented, so off I went. We played night basketball at Frank Roder's house because he had lights. Frank was Art Roder's son. (Yes, the same as Art's Grocery) I actually did go play basketball that night; I needed to have some degree of truth in what I said I was doing.

When it started to get dark, I told everyone playing ball that I was going home. I walked down the street about a block then cut across the street and around to the back of the equipment dealership. It was still light enough that I could see what I was doing. I climbed up the tractor tire, climbed into the window and onto the walk-way just as planned. It was dark inside the building. The only things I could see clearly were two lighted exit signs; one above the door to the outside and one to the front business area. As I slowly made my way toward the exit light to the business area door, I started feeling things I had felt once before. Those memories of Art's quickly disappeared, as the smell of rubber from all the tires got so strong I almost gagged and my eyes were burning.

Once inside the office area, the smell wasn't so bad. I had no time to waste; I went straight to the cash register. I would repeat my grocery store caper. However, when I got to the register I found it to be locked. I tried everything but nothing worked. All the planning had been for nothing.

Pling! Something had fallen from a shelf under the cash register and onto the floor.

I reached down and felt around in the dark. Suddenly, there it was a strange piece of metal on a chord. I wasn't sure what it was, so I went over and used the light from the pop machine to get a closer look. It looked like it might be some kind of key. It was round and had a key type handle on the end.

"Maybe it's the key to the cash register," I thought to myself.

I went back to the register and gave the key a try. It didn't work.

"The key has to be to something," I thought, as I looked around.

I went back to the pop machines to take another look at the key. That's when I noticed the symbol on the key handle. The pop machine! The key was to the pop machines. I quickly opened one of the machines. The cash box was almost overflowing. I went back behind the counter and got a paper bag to put the coin in. I only took half of what was in the cash box so no one would suspect anything. I opened the other machine and emptied it in the same manner. I calmly closed the machines, locked them, put the key back where I thought it belonged, and I walked out the side door.

As I lay in bed that night, I had a strong sensation come over me for the first time in my life. The "window caper" had been too easy. I went over and over in my mind how I had planned everything out. Then, I remembered what Dad had done for me when I had robbed Art's store. Somehow, he had prevented me from going to the reform school for boys. Why couldn't I sleep? Was my guardian angel speaking to me so I felt a sense of guilt, or was I just worried about what would happen to me if I got caught again? One thing I knew for sure; I wasn't taking the money to school.

The next day, I decided I couldn't risk somebody finding all that money around the house so I needed to find another place to hide it. I knew the perfect place; I would hide it on one of the pillars of the Chippewa River Bridge by the dam. No one would ever find it out there. I went down to the bridge. With the river flowing twenty feet below, I climbed onto the beam and out to the pillar. I slid the sack of money under the beam and crawled back to shore. I looked around to make sure nobody saw me. I would wait a week or so, then come back, and get some of the money to spend.

The week went slowly by. I thought about all that money under the bridge. What would I spend it on? A baseball glove, a bat, a fishing pole, or other things I didn't have. As it turned out, I never did get to spend that money. When I crawled back out to the pillar to retrieve my fortune, the money was gone.

"Where's my money?" I thought to myself, as I frantically looked around the pillar and under the beam.

My mind was racing away, as I surmised the situation. Some one must have seen me put the money out on the pillar. What if it was Ken or Carol or someone else that knows our family? What if they told my dad? What if? What if? One thing was certain, I couldn't go home!

I had run away from home many times before. I would always find somewhere safe and cozy to hide and sleep. One time, it was in a bunch of tires behind the Sinclair gas station. I can still smell the stinky rubber from those tires. Another time, it was amongst a pile of smelly Christmas trees at a friend's house. I would always get cold or hungry after a couple of hours of hiding. So, I would sneak into the house through the window above my bed, being ever so careful not to wake up Carol. Sometimes I got lucky; Dad would be too drunk to even notice that I had been missing. Ken and Carol always kept quiet because they didn't want Dad to get upset and go on a rampage. This time was different; I had done something terribly wrong and Dad would make me pay a big price if he found out.

There was a clump of bushes along Lake Lagoon that I had made into a fort earlier that year. That would be the perfect place to set up camp. To make sure I didn't get too cold or hungry this time, I hurried home to get supplies for my camp. Nobody was home. I put some bread and peanut butter into a bag along with a bottle of pop. I grabbed my pillow and a blanket from the bed, some clothes from the dresser, and my BB gun from the closet. With everything rolled up in the blanket, I looked around our cold, damp, basement house and said goodbye. I had all I needed to survive in the world on my own.

Camp was simple, but cozy. I had cleared out a section in the middle of the bushes, so it was difficult to see in or out of the fort. As the sun set and the moon rose in the sky, moonlight shown through the branches. I spread the blanket out and lay back, looked up at the star-filled sky and enjoyed the peacefulness. It was only a couple of hours after sundown when their shouting woke me up.

"Lanny!"

"Lanny, where are you? It's time to come home!"

Kenny and Carol, along with half the neighborhood, were out looking for me. Carol had seen that my pillow and blanket were gone along with the bread and peanut butter. She knew I had run away again. She had gotten a bunch of our friends together to look for me. I could see them across the lake from my camp in the bushes.

Several minutes passed, before suddenly from behind me I heard, "There you are, you little brat!"

I turned to see my brother standing with a flashlight shining in my face. "Why do you have to cause trouble all the time?"

"What do you care? You're not the one in trouble!" I snapped.

"When Dad's pissed at you, he's pissed at everyone!" Ken retorted. "We have to get you home before he gets home."

"You mean Dad doesn't know I ran away from home?"

"No," Ken answered. "Now let's go!"

We made it home before our dad. Ken and Carol questioned me as to why I wanted to run away from home all the time, even though I think they knew. We climbed into bed and lay awake wondering what kind of shape Dad would be in when he got home. We all fell asleep before he got home that night. I guess he never did find out about the "Broken Window Caper".

What was that strong sensation I had felt trying to fall asleep every night? Why had the money disappeared? I was sure nobody had seen me hide it. Was it irony, coincidence, misfortune, a blessing in disguise, or divine intervention? If the money had still been there and I had bought all the things I wanted, I would not have been able to explain to anyone, especially to Dad, where it all came from. Then, where would I have ended up?

Ruth Gamm

Ruth Saumer

Jill and Betty

Carol and Lanny

Lanny – Dad in basement house window

Lanny – Ken - Carol

Lanny and Ken

PART TWO
UP ON THE HILL

Chapter Five

A NEW LIFE

We moved "up on the hill" in the middle of my fifth grade year at Ramsey Elementary School. For the rest of the school year, I had to walk one mile from one end of town to the other to go to school. That was okay because I liked doing it. I had grown accustomed to walking to school while living in Smith Addition. Walking kept me away from home longer.

The home we moved into was one house away from the South end of Sixth Street. Across the road to the South and West, was Chinhinta Park. Down below the park hill, was the GTA grain elevator where Dad eventually worked until he retired. Beyond the elevator, was the Milwaukee Railroad Switch yard and highway 212. I had to cross the highway often to go to the grocery store, bowling alley, or fairgrounds.

Directly to the North of our home, was the abandoned Hillcrest Elementary School. Monte had built a new elementary school a couple of years before we moved up on the hill. I went to the new Sandford Elementary School for my sixth grade, which required about a mile walk each way. I had to walk about six blocks to go to church and on the way I could stop at my grandparents' home or my aunt and uncle's for a short visit and an occasional snack.

We lived at 504 South Sixth Street until my Junior Year in High School. It seemed like quite a step up for us after living in a basement house for so long. The home had a very steep gravel driveway without a garage. The yard was rather large and sloped toward the back. In the spring the front of the big white house was embraced with Lilacs and Babies Breath. The place had a personality of its own. The six years we lived there provided me with a new world and a new life; one of friends, school, sports, and love.

Our new home really wasn't new at all. It was an old house with some pretty neat, and not so neat, qualities. It had a crawl space basement with dirt walls and floor. I dreaded going into the basement crawl space to thaw out water pipes in the winter. There was a big open cistern in the middle of the space and you only had a couple feet to get around it. I always thought a monster lived in the cistern, just waiting for me to fall into it and provide him with a nice lunch. Two parlor stoves, in the living room and kitchen on the main floor, heated the home. Registers went up through the ceiling to the two second floor bedrooms. We would look down through the floor registers and watch the adults play cards at the kitchen table and at the same time we got a little warmth. The main floor also had a small bathroom, a small bedroom, and a laundry room. Across from the two second floor bedrooms was a storage room.

It was a lot more space than we were use to. Dad had the small bedroom on the main floor. Ken and I shared one of the up stair bedrooms. Carol was a teenager, and she finally had a room of her own. Carol's bedroom had a bay window that matched the living room below. From Carol's room, you could see most of the south end of town below the hill. I would often watch the stock-car races from her bay window.

We had spent most of a Saturday making the big move up from Smith Addition. My sister, Betty, and her husband, Donny, helped us with their pickup truck. As we turned the corner at the top of the hill with our last load, I saw some boys playing baseball on the school playground next to our new home. When we got the truck unloaded, I went around to the back of the house and watched the boys play ball. I had played ball in Smith Addition a few times over the years but to no great extent. In fact, I didn't even own a glove. As I watched the boys play, I could tell that they didn't just play baseball once in awhile. The three boys threw and hit the ball like nobody I had ever seen before.

It had been quite a day, and I was about to spend my first night sleeping with my brother in our new home.

"You wet the bed and I'll kill you!" Ken said, with a fist cocked, ready to hit me.

"I haven't wet the bed for years!" I replied smartly.

I crawled into bed and pulled the covers up around my neck. Ken got out his guitar, sat at the end of the bed and started to play some notes from a song called "Apache".

"I didn't know you could play that good," I commented.

"I can only play a couple of things," he replied.

I couldn't believe my ears when I heard him ask, "Do you want to learn how to play?"

Ken motioned me over to his side of the bed, as he pulled the guitar strap from around his neck. He had never asked me to do anything with him before.

"Wow! Would you really teach me?" I exclaimed.

"Sure. As much as I know, anyway," he laughed.

We sat on the edge of the bed playing the guitar until my fingers were too sore to play anymore, which probably wasn't all that long.

"That was really neat! Thanks." I said, as I crawled back under the covers.

"We'll do it again sometime." Ken replied.

"What a day this has been!" I thought to myself, as I lay in bed with all that had happened racing through my mind. Would I ever see the old basement house or my old friends again? I could see the boys playing ball on the playground next door. I wondered: Where do those boys live? Will they let me play with them? What will they think of me when they find out I'm not a very good baseball player? I felt my sore finger tips. I couldn't wait to play the guitar with Ken again; for me that moment will live on in my mind forever.

≈

Sunday came quickly after a good night's sleep. I was excited because we were invited to Grandma Florence and Grandpa Raymond Gamms' house for lunch. They only lived about five blocks from us on Fifth Street. Grandma Gamm was very special to me. I had been taking care of their house and lawn, as well as her church, for a couple of years. I mowed and raked the yards, washed windows, changed screens and storm windows, and shoveled snow from the sidewalks on both corner lots. It was a lot of work for a young boy, but Grandma always paid me well and made me feel important. It was a mile trek to their house from Smith Addition. Now it would only be a five block walk. Over the next few years, I made many stops on the way to church every Sunday and sat with Grandpa and his little Chihuahua dog, named Bitty. We watched Oral Roberts on television and Grandma gave me milk and cookies and Grandpa his coffee. Grandpa Raymond died a couple hours after one of those special visits.

When we were done visiting Grandma and Grandpa that Sunday, I thought I would take a chance and ask Dad a question.

"Would it be ok if I walked home?" I asked hesitantly.

"Why do you want to walk home?" Dad questioned.

"I want to see how long it takes to walk here when I have to come and do chores next Saturday," I answered.

"I guess that's a pretty good idea," Dad agreed. "Carol, why don't you walk home with Lanny to make sure he doesn't get lost on the way."

"I know the way home!" I exclaimed. "It's one block over to Sixth Street and then five blocks down to our house. How can I get lost?"

"Knowing you, you would find a way and we don't want to have to go looking for you," Dad said caringly, but with a little sarcasm in his voice.

I really did only want to know how long it took to walk home from Grandma's, so it was fine if Carol wanted to walk home with me. Grandma's house was on the way to the Junior-Senior High School, just three blocks away, so Carol wanted to see what her walk to school would be also.

"Let's go, Brother," Carol said, as she started walking down the sidewalk toward Sixth Street.

When we got to Sixth Street, we recognized the house on the far corner. Our cousins, the Veimans, had lived there a few years ago and had since moved to the North end of town.

"Do you remember when Robyn bit me in the arm?" I asked Carol.

"Did Robyn really bite you?" she questioned.

"I still have a scar to prove it!" I said, as I showed her my arm.

"Wow! That must have really hurt," Carol said, with a tint of sympathy in her voice. "You'll probably have that scar for life," she added. As it turned out, she was right.

We quietly continued our walk down Sixth Street, a trip I would make hundreds of times over the next six years. We were both studying every home along the way; they are still etched into my memory. Some of them belonged to friends that I had not made yet.

I finally broke the silence and asked Carol, "Do you think you'll like living here?"

"I don't know, "she said. "I guess so. I really like having a room of my own.–And the walk to school looks like it will be ok. "

"What about your friends in Smith Addition? Won't you miss them?" I asked.

"Yes," she sighed, and then added, "but I'll see them at school every day. I have classes with both Gloria and Diane."

"All my friends were older than me. I probably won't ever see them again," I retorted.

"Sure you will," Carol tried to encourage me.

The walk from Grandma's to home was short and didn't take long at all. Dad was surprised when he saw us walk in through the front door.

"How was the walk home? Carol, are you going to be okay walking to school?" he asked.

"It should be fine, Dad," she replied.

"They don't have a school bus that goes to Ramsey from here, Lanny. Do you think you can walk to there from here? It's at the other end of Sixth Street." I couldn't believe my ears; Dad was actually asking me for my opinion. Who was this guy?

I didn't hesitate to answer, "Sure I can. I hate riding the school bus anyway."

For the last three months of my fifth grade year, I walked the two miles to Ramsey Elementary School and back home. I loved the freedom! I think I also liked the respect my dad gave me for making that walk every day.

Later on that Sunday, I looked out the back door of our house. There they were, the three boys playing baseball again. Dad was taking a nap on the couch, so I quietly slipped out the back door. I slowly made my way over to the playground and sat on one of the swings. I watched with envy, as the boys played ball. Finally, one of the boys stopped and looked over at me.

"Do you want to play with us?" he yelled. "We could use another player."

"I don't have a glove or anything!" I gave an excuse not to play and demonstrate my lack of athletic ability.

"That's all right. We have extra gloves and you can use our bats!" the boy replied.

"Ok, I guess I can play," I mumbled, as I slowly walked toward the boys. I figured it wouldn't be long before they knew how bad I was and wouldn't want me to play anymore, but I would give it a shot anyhow.

"What's your name?" the short boy who had called me over asked. He then introduced himself, "I'm Larry Davis. I live across the street from you."

"I'm Lanny Saumer," I answered.

"I'm Richard Johnson. I live in the duplex next door to you," said a tall skinny red headed boy.

"And I'm Brian Harding. I live in that house over there," added a tall and husky boy.

"What position do you like to play Lanny?" Larry asked.

"I don't know. I haven't played much ball. I'm not very good," was all I could say.

"That's OK. We play work up. So, you end up playing outfield, then first base, then pitcher, and then you get to bat," explained Larry. "You get to bat until you're put out. Then everyone rotates positions."

"I think I understand," I said.

"Good, you take the outfield," Larry suggested.

That suggestion turned out to be a disaster. After I missed a dozen fly balls and grounders, Larry was getting tired of running the bases, Brian was tired of pitching to Larry, and Richard was tired of standing around doing nothing.

"This isn't working very well!" Larry finally acknowledged.

"You were right when you said you aren't very good!" Brian added.

Larry came to my rescue, "He'll be OK. He just needs a little practice."

"Hey, why don't we play 500?" Richard suggested. "We can practice catching fly balls. Do you know how to play 500 Lanny?"

"I've played it a few times," I replied.

"Sounds good!" said Larry. "Let's play! Richard, it was your idea. Why don't you bat first?"

Richard grabbed a bat and the three of us went to the outfield. Richard hit a high fly ball and Brian ran over and caught it.

"That's 100 for Brian!" Richard called out.

How was I ever going to get 500 points against Brian and Larry? I hadn't caught a fly ball all day. Eventually, Brian had earned his 500 points and got to be the batter. Richard came out into the outfield, and we started a new game. It turned out that Richard couldn't catch a fly ball much better than me. So it wasn't long before Larry had 500 points and became the batter. The first ball he hit came right toward me. It wasn't all that high, just a little pop-up. I saw the ball clearly, ran up a few feet and caught it.

"That's 100 for Lanny!" Larry called out.

That was music to my ears! It turned out to be the only ball I caught that day. Brian was first to get to 500 points and earn the right to be batter again.

"Hey Lanny, I have to get home. Why don't you bat for me?" Brian yelled over to me.

"All right, thanks!" I shouted.

As I ran up to be the batter, Larry smiled at me and said, "Show us your stuff Saumer!"

Although I couldn't field the ball very well, I knew I could hit it. I had spent hours hitting rocks along the Chippewa River bank. Crack! I hit my first ball. Larry and Richard turned and watched the ball go over the fence.

"I'd like to see that again!" Larry shouted, as he threw the ball back to me.

Crack! I sent another ball flying over the fence.

Richard and Larry were laughing and "high fiving" one another. Then Richard yelled, "Hey, that's great, but now let up and hit some so we can catch them."

It really pumped me up to hear them laughing and hear him say that. I knew they were going to be good friends. As I retrieved the ball and turned back to go to home plate and hit the next ball, I saw a figure with a bike at the top of the hill watching us. I waved at him and motioned him to come over. Wayne got on his bike, turned, and disappeared down the hill. I only remember seeing Wayne a couple of times at school after that day. My old friend wasn't to be part of my new life.

Chapter Six

STRANGERS

$\mathcal{M}$inneapolis, Minnesota, was a huge city for a ten year old boy from the little farming town of Montevideo. Each summer I would spend a couple of weeks in Minneapolis with my sister Jill, her husband Bunky, and their two infant kids, Theresa and Art. The big city had always been a little scary to me. I didn't like the crowds of people down town, and I didn't understand the street lights very well. I remember the strong smell of diesel fuel from the buses that constantly went by Jill's apartment. She warned me that if I got on the wrong bus I might not get back home, so I never took the bus anywhere. She also warned me not to talk to strangers, or take anything from them. I spent a lot of my time safely watching television because they had channels with shows we didn't get back home.

About a block uptown and around the corner was a building where blind people made brooms. I could stand and watch them through the big window in front of the building. I remember being fascinated by how blind people could do their work so effortlessly. I would close my eyes and pretend to be blind and try to do some of the things they did. That respect for the abilities of blind people has stuck with me.

A couple of girls lived in an apartment or two down the street. They were actually pretty nice to me, but they were girls, so I didn't have much to do with them. Sometimes, I would torment them when they played Hop-Scotch on the side walk. Teasing them was just something for me to do.

Once in awhile, I would get outside and play in the back alley with a black boy from the apartment below. We were close to the same age and had one big thing in common— we both liked to smoke. I would steal cigarettes from my sister and he would steal them from his mother. We would meet in the back alley and go between the garages and light up. Aside from that, we didn't do much together because his mother wouldn't allow him to go anywhere.

After a few days of total boredom, I decided to get a little braver. We had finished lunch, and Jill was doing some laundry while the kids were napping. I was left pretty much on my own for the afternoon.

"Can I go outside for awhile?" I asked Jill.

"Sure. You be careful! Stay out of the street and remember, don't talk to strangers!" she habitually reminded me.

"I'll be careful!" I promised her.

"And don't be late for supper!" she ordered.

I looked up the street. The girls weren't playing outside. I walked around to the back of the apartment. I hung around and waited for Jimmy to come out to have a couple of smokes. After smoking a few cigarettes by myself, I decided to expand my horizon a little.

I went back to the front of the apartment and started to walk down the street. I walked past the apartment where the girls lived and went all the way to the corner.

"That was no big deal!" I thought to myself.

I waited for the stop light to turn green. I crossed the street and continued on my journey. I didn't know where I was going. I figured that if I just stayed on this street, I could turn around and go back to the apartment without any problem at all. I kept on walking, crossing one intersection after another. Then, there it was, a park like I had never seen before in my life. It was huge. People were everywhere and the traffic was thick. As I waited for the traffic light to turn green, I looked across the street and studied the park. Off to the left was a playground area with swings, teeter-totters, and monkey bars. That looked like a fun and safe place to go.

Swinging just to swing never made much sense to me; it was actually a little boring. So, like all boys tend to do, I made up games while I was swinging. It was fun to see how far I could parachute out of my dive bomber swing. A lot of kids were waiting to play on the equipment, so I didn't get to play the way I was accustomed. Every time I parachuted out of my swing, some other kid would take it before I could get back. I got pretty dizzy spinning around over and over in my swing, and I gave it up.

The park had a set of horizontal monkey bars just like the ones on my Hillcrest playground back home. I was the master of this piece of equipment. I could zip across the ladder skipping every other rod or even every two rods. Like the swings, there was quite a crowd of kids waiting their turn to get on the monkey bars. After attempting a few trips across the bars, I got frustrated. I couldn't do anything because of the crowd. Another set of monkey bars only had kids playing on them on one end. I ran over to the empty end of the monkey bars and climbed the ladder. I would show these kids how to run this ladder. I jumped out and grabbed the third rod. I never made it to the sixth rod.

As it turned out, the reason nobody was playing on that end of the monkey bars was because there were two loose rods at that end. The kids that played in the park all the time knew not to play on that end of the bars. When I grabbed hold of the third rod, which was loose, my hand slipped off and my body's momentum flung my legs up into the air, and I fell to the ground hitting the back of my head. The lights went out! When I finally woke up, there was a crowd gathered around me.

"Are you OK?" I heard someone say.

"Just lie still, don't you move!" another person ordered.

"Should somebody call for an ambulance?" a lady asked.

"No! Don't call for an ambulance! I'm OK!" I exclaimed.

"I don't know. You were out for quite awhile," the lady said. "Can I give you a ride home?" she added.

All I could think about was how much trouble I would be in if my sister found out that I had walked all the way down to this park and had gotten hurt.

"No! I'm not supposed to talk to strangers!" I exclaimed.

I got up and started walking. I knew where I was and where I had to go, so I figured I was okay. By the time I got back to the apartment, I was feeling well, and I was back in time for supper. Somehow, I had managed to escape another tragedy. There was no need for Jill to ever find out what had happened.

Chapter Seven
TIME TO QUIT

Hillcrest School was a neat old abandoned building. I spent hours using it to practice baseball by myself. I drew a rectangle on the wall to represent the strike zone. Over the years, I threw thousands of balls at that school to work on my control and fielding. I never did develop into anything special in baseball, but I did get to be a lot better, thanks to that old building.

Because of their unique structure, the two back doors of the abandoned building also served a function for me. Above the doorway to each air-lock entry, was a sunken flat roof with a wall around it. I had often wondered what it was like above the doors. One evening, I climbed up the corner of one of the entries to gain access to the roof area about ten or twelve feet above the ground. Once I climbed over the wall and onto the roof, I made a discovery. If you sat down on the roof, nobody could see you behind the wall. Nobody else would ever dare to climb up the corner of the building to get onto the entry roof. What a great hide-away!

Although we had lived on the hill for a couple of years, and I enjoyed a much better life than the one I had in Smith Addition, I didn't give up some of my old behaviors. About every two weeks, Dad would buy a new carton of cigarettes, take one pack out, and he would place the carton in a cupboard above the kitchen sink. The next day, while Dad was at work, I would cleverly slide all the packs out of the carton, take one pack for myself, and I would put the rest back in the carton so it looked like only one pack was gone. By the time Dad got to the end of the carton, he never knew what had happened. My Hillcrest hide-away was the perfect place to go smoke a couple of cigarettes without anyone ever seeing me. I hid my cigarettes and lighter there. As often as we played football or baseball on the playground, and as tempting as it was, I never let anyone know about my secret. When we finished with practice, and everyone else went home, I went back to the school, climbed up into my hide-away, and had a smoke. I couldn't risk my friends finding out about my hide-away and that I smoked. I didn't want to quit smoking and I liked having my neighborhood friends.

My first athletic injury was a sprained shoulder I got playing seventh grade flag football. I really hadn't been hurt that bad, but the coach took me to the doctor, and as a result, my arm was in a sling for three weeks. I had finished my chores, and Dad was working his usual Saturday morning shift at the GTA elevator below the hill. The sling on my arm prevented me from doing too much. I decided to walk over to the playground and watch my friends play football. When I got there Brian, Larry, and Richard were sitting on the school lawn.

"What's up, guys? Why aren't you playing football?"

"We're thinking about going hunting out at the old drive-in theater," Larry said.

"What's there to hunt for out there?" I asked.

"I saw some geese there this morning," Brian answered.

"We're going to go there this afternoon after lunch," Larry said as he stood up. "Do you want to come along?"

"I don't have a gun," I confessed. "Besides, I wouldn't be much good with my stupid arm."

"Well, if you want to go you can use my brother's Twenty Gauge," Brian said. "You'll have to furnish your own shells though."

"We're going to meet at my place at one o'clock and ride our bikes out to the drive-in," Larry added. "Even if you can't hunt, why don't you just come along?"

Since it was my left arm that was in a sling, I figured I could shoot a gun. I wanted to go hunting in the worst way. However, even if I had money to buy shells for the gun, Dad would never let me go. But then I realized my dad didn't need to know. I could tell him I was going to do something with another friend that lived by Sandford Elementary School. All I needed to do was figure out how to get some shells. I had no clue as to how much they cost.

The best place in town to get sporting good equipment was the Montgomery Ward store. I had purchased many things there over the years without ever spending a dime by getting the five finger discount. This would have to be another one of those times. When I entered the store, I couldn't believe my eyes. Right inside the door were the shotgun shells. I didn't even have to look for them. But it wasn't as easy as it first appeared. It was important to make sure I got the right shells. After a few minutes of looking, I finally spotted the twenty gauge shells. I walked past them as I gazed around the store to see if anyone was watching. I went over and fumbled around looking at some fishing lures. I thought to myself, do I really want to do this? I've never really hunted anything in my life. How was I going to pull this off with my friends? If I don't go hunting they might not like me as much and they wouldn't ask me to go again. I sauntered back over to the shotgun shells. I took a last look around and slid a box of shells into my sling. After a minute or so of pretending to look at shells, I made my way to the door.

I was only a few feet out the door when I heard, "Just a minute young man!"

I stopped and turned. "Are you talking to me?"

"Yes, I am. What do you have in your sling?" the man asked as he grabbed me by the shoulder, reached into the sling, and drew out the box of shells. "I think you better come with me!"

The man took me back into the store. As he escorted me through the store, I could sense all kinds of people were watching. Where did they all come from? We made our way down a flight of stairs to an office in the basement.

"Sit here while I get the manager!" the man ordered.

It had finally happened, I had gotten caught stealing. I imagined all sorts of things while I sat in that office: The police were coming to put me in handcuffs and haul me off to jail. I was good as dead. Dad would give me the whipping of my life and send me off to reform school. I would never see my friends again.

The manager was a big man, bigger than my dad. "It seems we've got a problem here, young man," he said as he closed the door behind him. "What's you name?"

"Lanny Saumer," I whimpered.

The man looked at me like he was puzzled about something. "You're not Herb Saumer's boy are you?"

I knew I was in real trouble now. The man knows Dad. "Yes, Sir," I replied. "Do you know my dad?"

"I sure do. We used to be good hunting buddies before your mom died. Your dad had one of the best hunting dogs around. A beautiful Irish Setter just like this one," he explained as he took a picture of his own dog off the shelf above his desk to show me.

I figured I would play the sympathy card in hopes that the man would let me off easy. "He doesn't hunt and fish anymore. He spends most of his time working and drinking. We never have money for anything we want."

"I'm sorry to hear that. Your dad's a good man. I'm disappointed that his son feels he needs to steal to get what he wants."

My heart sunk to my feet. I had never heard anyone ever call my father a "good man" before. Dad had told me stories about his hunting and fishing days. I always thought they were just stories that he had made up. Here I was, sitting in this stranger's office, hearing stories about him and Dad hunting together years ago. A combination of pride and shame swept through my body, as I realized how great a man my dad had once been and what he had become.

"Out of respect for your dad, this is what we're going to do," the manager explained. "You're going to go straight home and stay there. When your dad gets home you tell him what you did today. I'll let him deal with you, and I won't report you to the police." The man handed me a piece of paper with his name and phone number on it. "Have your dad call me after you tell him everything. If I don't hear from him by Monday, I'll have to report you to the police. Do you understand, Lanny?"

"Yes, Sir," I said with a feeling of reluctance. This was a "lose-lose" situation. Either I get a beating and grounded for life, or I get put in jail and sent to reform school.

"If you follow through with this plan, I'll ask your dad to let me take you hunting with me and my dog in a couple of weeks. How's that sound?"

I couldn't believe my ears. "That sounds great," I agreed, feeling a little puzzled.

The morning seemed to last forever. The time in the manager's office had only been a half hour or so. As I made the long walk home, I spun everything over in my mind: What the man had said about my dad. The promise I had made to the man. What was I going to say to Dad when he got home? What was I going to tell my friends as to why I couldn't go hunting with them?

I was putting away the last of the dishes I had just washed, when I heard Dad walk in through the front door. I heard him fumbling around in the living room. I stayed in the kitchen. I really didn't want to see him. I felt a knot in the pit of my stomach as he appeared in the kitchen doorway. "You're home?" Dad asked uncaringly. "I thought you would be off with your buddies somewhere." He went into his room next to the kitchen.

"What do you want for supper?" I called out to him.

"I don't care. Whatever you want to make is fine. Wake me when it's ready," he replied.

I proceeded to make some rice with raisins, which just happened to be one of Dad's favorites. When it was time, I called Dad out to eat. He sure appeared to be in a good mood. I didn't want to upset the applecart. I just went along as if nothing was wrong.

We had finished eating and I was clearing the table when Dad finally asked the big question. "Just what did you do today, Lanny?"

"Oh, nothing much, just hung out with the guys," I replied.

"Yeah, but what'd you do? Play football? Go down town?" He inquired.

"I watched the guys play football for awhile and then we went down town and played cards."

"Is that all you did?"

Oh, Oh! He wouldn't be drilling me like this if he didn't know. He was giving me every opportunity to fess up. I stuck to my story, "That's about it." I waited for all hell to break loose.

"Isn't there something you want to tell me, Lanny?" Dad asked in a soft, caring voice.

I was confused. If he knew, why wasn't he upset? Maybe he didn't know. "No, I don't have anything to tell you."

Then it came, like a disease silently catching up with you, "Didn't something happen at the Ward store today?"

I was dead. "Oh Yeah, I forgot. I...," I started to explain.

Before I got out another word, Dad stood up and looked at me with a cold stare and said, "Son, if you can forget what you did today, then I guess there's no hope for you." He turned, went into the living room and turned on the television.

I sat in the kitchen, not knowing what to do. Where is the beating, the lecture, or the grounding? I finally got up enough nerve and went into the living room and sat down in the chair next to Dad lying on the sofa. With tears running down my cheeks, I apologized, "I'm sorry, Dad. I didn't really forget what I did today. I was just afraid to tell you."

"Good luck with your life, Lanny. I won't visit you in prison!"

Nothing more was said to each other about that day for many years. I never did get to go hunting with the manager from Wards. As for my friends, well that didn't turn out too good. It was shortly after dinner when someone knocked at the back door. It was Richard. We sat on the back steps and he told me about the big hunting trip. He told me about how much fun they had sneaking up on the geese and trying to shoot them. They didn't kill any but they had a blast. I was feeling envious, when all of a sudden Richard let me have it. "We know what you did yesterday, Lanny! My mom was in the store when they caught you. I'm not allowed to do anything with you anymore."

Richard got up and started to walk away. He turned and looked back at me and informed me, "By the way, I also know about your smoking cigarettes above the door of the school! I just don't want to be your friend anymore!"

I continued to sit on the back steps thinking about the past two days. What did it all mean? Nobody was really mad at me. They had just given up on me. Was Dad right? If I didn't change my ways, was I going to end up in prison? Was I going to lose all my friends? The more I thought, the more I realized I was sick of all my old ways. It was "time to quit!"

I got up from the steps and went over to my hide-away. I climbed up to the roof, gathered up all my supplies, and climbed back down. I took the supplies to our burn barrel, started a fire, and I dumped everything into the fire.

It would be 1968 before I would ever smoke another cigarette. I have never stolen anything in my life again. I have never spent a day behind bars. And, I have made many great friends over the years. Most of them would find my stories hard to believe, based upon the Lanny they now know. However, I think we can all say, "We are who we are today because of our total past." We all have our own little stories. As we go through life, we make countless choices and those choices impact our life forever.

Chapter Eight
LESSONS ON THE FARM

*N*othing builds a person's character like the lessons learned on the farm. I was very fortunate to have two sisters who each married a farmer. I loved it on the farm. In my younger years, I picked rocks and pulled weeds in the fields on Betty's and Donny's farm. As I got older, I started baling hay and eventually got to drive tractors on Carol's and LeRoy's farm. There were always animal chores to do. However, the farm wasn't just a great place to work; it was also a great place to play. It was easy to escape and find something to do in the barn, in one of the other buildings, on a piece of equipment, or in the grove that surrounded the farm site.

The barn on Betty's farm proved to be the place where I managed to get into the most trouble. Not that I did things that were wrong, but I did things that often resulted in me getting hurt. If Betty had known, I probably would not have been allowed to play in the barn. The most fascinating part of the barn was the hayloft. The farm had once been a dairy farm before Betty and Donny moved there. While I spent the summers on their farm, the livestock was mostly pigs, chickens, and a few beef cows. We never had milking chores to do. Whatever the livestock, there seemed to always be a fair amount of hay in the barn.

Each end of the hayloft had a big set of doors. One end was for loading the hay into the loft and the other end was for throwing bales down to feed the cattle in the feed-lot.

When I got back the summer I had my little incident with strangers at Jill's, I went out to Betty's to spend a couple of weeks. One evening, I was given the chore to throw a few bales of hay down into the feed-lot crib before the cattle came from the pasture. It was a chore I had done many times and enjoyed doing because I always made a game of it. After I threw down half a dozen bales or so, I would go down and fluff up the hay in the crib with a pitch fork. Then I would go back up into the loft and jump down into the crib a few times before the cattle would get there.

That evening didn't turn out as usual. While I was fluffing up the hay in the crib, I noticed a bale had bounced out of the crib and onto the ground. Donny didn't like the cattle to eat hay off the ground because they could ingest bad things, like nails and wire. I lay the pitch fork down and jumped out of the crib onto the ground. The string on the bail had broken, so I had to throw the hay up into the crib loose. Once I got the hay cleaned up off the ground, I was good to go. I looked down at the pasture and saw that the cattle were on their way like clock work. I ran back up into the barn hay-loft, went to the open door, and performed my usual butt flop into the hay crib.

"Practice good safety, pay attention to what you're doing." Some lessons in life are learned the hard way. This was a painful lesson. I hadn't paid attention to what I was doing. I had forgotten that I had laid the pitchfork down in the hay crib and hadn't picked it up and put it back in the barn. When I landed on the hay, two of the tines of the pitchfork stuck me in the buttocks. One of the tines actually went up into my anus, leaving a lifelong scar. The other tine just scratched the side of by butt. Somebody was looking out for me that day. Out of embarrassment, I don't think I ever said anything to anyone about the incident.

≈

A summer or two later, I was horsing around in the hayloft again. I was playing pirate. I would swing on the rope for the bale sling. The bale sling was a rope that hung down from a movable pulley that ran along the big center beam at the peak of the barn roof. It was used to move a bale of hay to place it on the top of a stack that might be fifteen or twenty feet high. I learned another painful lesson that day while swinging from one side of the barn to the other, pretending to be a pirate. "Be aware of your surroundings." What I wasn't aware of that day was that one of the hatch doors in the floor had been left open. At the completion of one of my swings, I slid down the back side of the pile of hay and slid right through the door in the floor. The pain came when I hit my head on the cement feeding trough below. I don't know how long I was knocked out. I remember waking up in the barn, in a lot of pain, with quite a bump on my head. I went to the house and told Betty what had happened. She was a nurse and knew what to do. I would be reminded of that lesson a couple of years later.

Betty and Donny gave me a BB gun for Christmas when I was in the sixth or seventh grade. I would take my BB gun with me to the farm and go around the grove shooting at things. A tin can on top of a fence post was the most common target. As I got older, my BB gun didn't have the same appeal to me. I think I was probably fourteen, when Donny took me out to the grove and let me shoot his 22 caliber rifle. That was really neat. We set up cans on a fallen tree trunk and picked them off one by one. It was one of a few times I remember doing anything with Donny besides work. Once in awhile we would go into town and shoot pool.

Thanksgiving was always a good time out on the farm. Betty would make a huge meal and everyone would stuff themselves. The adults would always end up playing penny- ante poker. I was kind of caught in the middle, too old for my nieces and nephews and too young for the adults. I didn't have my BB gun, so I asked Donny if I could use his 22 to go and shoot targets. He always liked it when I showed signs of growing up, so he let me use his rifle. "Remember, never shoot toward the house!" he reminded me, as he handed me the rifle and a box of shells.

I went out to the grove where we always shot targets and blasted away. After awhile I started to get a little bored. I decided to go on a real hunt for a squirrel or rabbit. I could never get close enough with my BB gun, but with the 22 rifle I didn't need to get so close. I was set to bag my first real game.

I had just crossed the road when I saw the rabbit out of the corner of my eye. He had stopped, making a target big as life. I slowly lifted the rifle to my shoulder, being careful not to spook the "big game". I set the rifle sights clearly on the rabbit. I could feel my heart pounding in my chest. I took a deep breath. He was as good as gone. I squeezed the trigger. I saw a flash of leaves about a foot in front of the rabbit, followed instantly with a loud smack. I watched the rabbit run for his life.

I walked up to where the rabbit had been sitting as a target. I saw clearly where the 22 bullet had hit the ground. I brushed the leaves aside only to see the top of a huge rock with a white mark on it. The bullet had ricocheted off the rock. I instantly remembered the loud smack that sounded right after the bullet hit the ground. What did the bullet end up hitting? As I stood up, I remembered the last words Donny had said to me. I looked back to where I had taken the shot. There were about fifty yards of grove, ten yards of lawn, and then the house. I walked toward the house with my worst fears rushing through my mind. Had the bullet hit the house? If so, how much damage had I done? What would Donny say?

When I reached the house, I looked all around. I couldn't see any major damage. There were no broken windows. That was a relief. Then I saw where the bullet had hit, about six inches below one of the windows. A piece of the white painted siding had a small hole, the size of a dime in it. I could see the shiny end of the bullet embedded in the hole. I looked in the window and saw the living room was empty.

When I went into the house, nobody said a word to me. I knew I was in the clear, and I was so thankful nobody got hurt. I would never forget the lesson I learned that day; a lesson taught in every required hunter safety class today, "Be sure of your target and beyond".

Chapter Nine
ADOLESCENCE

*J*unior high school is a tough time for teenagers. Everything changes from elementary school. You have a different teacher for each subject, you move from one classroom to another, and you start traveling by school bus to other towns to play against them in sports. And of course, boys and girls start expressing an interest in each other.

The only problem the different classes and teachers presented for me was being tardy a lot over the years. I spent a fair amount of time in Vice Principal Neihart's office. I loved the trips to other towns to play sports. It was like the big boys. And sports meant more to me than just about anything. I used sports as a crutch when I messed up a couple of girlfriend relationships in junior high, which led me to be quite shy and introverted in high school. I made it clear to all my friends that I felt girls were simply too big a distraction. The real truth was I didn't want to risk being rejected again.

My relationship with Janet actually started as far back as third grade. I remember one of the last days of school at Sibley Elementary School. During recess, Janet asked me which school I would be transferring to for fourth grade since Sibley only went through third. I told her I would be going to Ramsey. She told me she would be going to Sandford and that she would miss me. I doubt that there is a man alive that doesn't remember the first time a girl told him that she would miss him.

Janet and I had gone our separate ways from Sibley Elementary School, but during the next few summers we would cross paths once in awhile at the community swimming pool. Sometimes, I actually went to the pool looking for her. One day while we were playing with our friends in the pool, I told Janet that I had moved up on the hill and that I would be transferring to Sandford for sixth grade.

She gave me a beautiful smile and said, "That's great, Lanny. Where do you live now?"

"We moved to South Sixth Street right by the old Hillcrest School."

"I only live three blocks from there!" Janet exclaimed. "I live on Fifth Street."

Her excitement flustered me, and all I could think of to say was, "I guess that kind of makes us neighbors."

We ended up in the same room in sixth grade. Sometimes we would play a sort of cat and mouse game walking home from school. Whoever got ahead a block would walk slower, so the other could catch up. It was our way of saying, "I like you." It was sweet and innocent.

In junior high our relationship graduated to a slightly higher level. It was common practice for seventh and eighth grade girls to throw what they called couples' parties. I was invited to a half dozen of those parties. Each time Janet and I were considered a couple. By night's end, we would usually have danced a couple times. Usually during those parties, the guys would hang out together and the girls would hang out together. The boys were mostly interested in eating.

In the spring, each grade would have a school dance. I had been walking Janet home from school for weeks and had not asked her to the dance. Finally, about three or four days before the dance, I called her on the telephone and asked her to the dance. She told me she was sorry, but I was too late. Someone else had asked her the day before and she had said yes. Janet continued dating that boy throughout high school and eventually married him. My wife, Karen, and I are good friends with them today. Karen and Janet usually have a nice visit at our class reunions. Karen has probably heard this story from Janet's viewpoint.

≈

The following summer I made another feeble attempt at a love connection. I went to Bible Camp with my best friend, David. Bible Camp was like nothing I had ever experienced before. I was away from home and family. David and I were the only two in camp from Montevideo. After a few days we connected with a couple of girls from Benson, Minnesota. We would meet them at the nightly campfires for sing-a-longs. They would come and watch us play softball, we would go and watch them play tennis, and during the second week of camp, the four of us ate together.

When camp ended we all exchanged addresses and said our goodbyes. We promised to write and make arrangements to see each other. We all followed through with that promise. David and Wendy wrote to each other. Jean and I wrote to each other several times.

One day, later that summer, Jean and Wendy came to Montevideo on a shopping trip with their mothers. David and I met them at the park and we spent the afternoon together. It was a beautiful day so we walked around the park holding hands, laughing, and talking. What a great two or three hours! As we were getting ready to leave the park, Jean gave me a kiss and a hug. I made a rather clumsy attempt at a hug and kiss back. I must admit, she had me hook, line, and sinker. We continued to write to each other on almost a daily basis.

In our freshman year of football, we were scheduled to play Benson at Benson. David and I made arrangements with Wendy and Jean to meet them after the game for a few minutes. David and I both had a great game that night and figured the girls would be impressed. As we walked toward the Benson bus, I saw Jean. She was with one of the Benson players and bam, she gave him a kiss.

David came over and told me that he had gotten the same message from Wendy. Those Benson Tramps!

For many years I protected myself from getting hurt like that again. I dedicated myself to sports and school. I didn't get involved with another girl for five years. At the end of our freshman year, David moved to Aitkin, MN. Being the handsome jock that he was, I'm sure he did just fine.

By the time I was in the ninth grade, I had been driving tractors and trucks for a couple of years. That was one of the great lessons on the farm. The common practice was to take "Behind the Wheel Driver Education" the summer after your ninth grade year. The only problem was that the course required a pretty hefty fee to be paid before your first day of driving. Knowing very well that Dad would not have the money to pay for the course, I brought home the registration form anyway. I promised Dad that I would save up my babysitting money to pay for the course. He complained about how his car insurance payment would go up when I became a licensed driver. I promised I would pay the difference in the insurance payment. He finally consented and signed the registration papers.

By the time my two weeks of "Behind the Wheel Driver Education" came around, I had not saved up enough money to pay the fee. I told my instructor, Mr. Morsetter, that I only had half of the fee and that I could pay the second half at the beginning of the second week of lessons after I earned the money babysitting. He was a kind old man and knew our family situation, so he agreed. Driving a brand new 1965 Ford Galaxy 500 was a real treat. Dad had a 1957 Ford with a stick-shift transmission, and the pickup truck on the farm also had a stick-shift. Driving the Driver's Ed. Car with an automatic transmission was a piece of cake. Plus, I got the added bonus of having two of the nicest girls in my class as driving partners. Life just didn't get any better!

Every Monday, before Dad got home from work, I walked about half a mile to Tillman's Grocery Store and purchase groceries for the week. It was a chore that I didn't mind because Dad would let me get a snack to eat on the way back home. I was tired from playing tennis all afternoon and was late getting home. It would be impossible to go to the store and back before Dad got home. Dad's car was in the driveway and the keys were in the kitchen. Problem solved. I'd take the car.

The trip to and from the grocery store went just fine. My biggest problem was driving that car up our steep driveway. The sharp turn into the driveway prevented me from getting any kind of run at it. I had to come to almost a complete stop at the bottom of the driveway hill, pop the clutch, and step on the gas without killing the engine. After the third or fourth attempt, I finally made the assent to the top of the driveway and slammed on the brakes to try to park the car in the same spot. Time was running out. Dad would be home any minute. I turned off the engine, got out of the car, grabbed the groceries, and ran into the house.

"Where in the hell is the car?" I heard Dad yell as he entered the front door.

"What do you mean?" I asked from the kitchen, where I had finished putting the groceries away and was starting to prepare supper.

"The car's not in the driveway!" Dad exclaimed.

"It was there when I got home from the store," I explained.

"Well, it's not there now! —What the hell! How did that happen?" Dad was frantic as he ran to the back door and looked out the window.

"What's wrong?" I asked, as I joined him at the window.

When I looked out the window, I realized what I had done and hadn't done. I didn't put the emergency brake on and had managed to leave the car in neutral. The car had rolled down the back yard and had crashed into a telephone pole. "How did that happen?" I questioned innocently.

"I don't know. I must have forgotten to put the emergency brake on," Dad replied with a puzzled tone in his voice.

We walked down to the car. The left front fender and headlamp were smashed. After looking the car over, Dad looked at me and said, "I think I can drive this out of here. Go up to the house and get the keys."

As I ran back to the house, I was feeling sick to my stomach. I was afraid Dad would figure out what really had happened. I would never get my driver's license. When I returned with the keys, I was surprised at how calm my dad had become. He simply said, "Let this be a good lesson for you, Lanny. Always remember to put the emergency brake on and make sure the car is in gear when you park."

Dad drove the car out and parked it in his usual spot. He got out of the car and looked around where he had parked, and then he looked down the driveway. I wondered if he saw anything. I walked up the back hill of the yard and joined him by the car. There they were, big as life, the tire marks from where I had spun the wheels trying to get up the driveway hill. Dad never said a word.

I didn't get my driver's license that summer. When I returned for my lesson on Tuesday, Mr. Morsetter asked me for the second half of my fees. I didn't have it, so it was the end of my lessons. I guess I really wasn't ready to be driving yet anyway. I repeated Driver's Ed and got my license the next summer.

The family has always viewed the '57 Ford incident as a great mystery. Mystery solved!

Chapter Ten

COLLEGE BOUND

*D*uring my junior year in high school, we moved to a home on Eleventh Street, which was about a half mile from the old junior/senior high school and a half mile from the new senior high school. I walked to the old school my junior year but had the luxury of driving Dad's '57 Ford Falcon to the new school most of my senior year. That made it possible for me to get home from football, wrestling, and baseball practices quicker, so I could have supper ready for Dad when he got home from work. I thought it was a pretty good deal; I was one of only a few Jocks that had his own car. Eleventh Street provided me with a modern home, a father who was becoming more loving, and a life dedicated to school and sports.

Spending the summer working on a line crew in the "Bad Lands" of North Dakota helped me to grow up; it was the key to my great senior year. Sister Jill had divorced Bunky several years before and moved into a home next to us on Sixth Street with her two children, Theresa and Art, whom I would always babysit when I was in junior high school. While I was in tenth grade, she married a man named Harvey. He was a "Lineman" for an electrical company out of Dickinson, North Dakota, so they moved to the small town of Taylor, about twenty miles from

Dickinson. Harvey and I got along very well. The summer before my senior year, he invited me to come up and work with him on his line crew. The job required me to walk about two or three miles through rugged terrain and dig three feet down all around the base of each power pole on the line. Harvey would follow me, inspect the pole, and either reject it or accept it for treatment. Another person followed Harvey and treated each pole that had been marked for treatment. It was a tough job, and my Guardian Angel came to my rescue a couple of times that summer. But, all that walking in North Dakota built up my leg muscles and got me into great shape for football that fall. Also, I managed to put some of my hard earned money from that summer into a savings account and was able to return to school with a good supply of new clothes for the first time in my life.

Remember when I said I had learned my lesson about being aware of your surroundings? I guess I hadn't learned it very well. One day, while working on the line crew in those "Bad Lands" of North Dakota, I found out how fast I could really run. I had done several poles and was quite a distance ahead of Harvey. The pole I was working on was in the middle of a cow pasture about two hundred feet from the gravel road. I was just about finished digging when I heard a snort and a scraping of the ground. To my surprise, I turned to find a huge bull standing next to a water trough about one hundred feet from me. He had either come to see what all the commotion was about or to simply get a drink. He was looking right at me and was not a happy camper. He snorted and stomped his foot again. I grabbed my shovel and started running for the road. That proved to be the wrong move. The bull came after me, and I literally ran for my life. I made it to the fence, climbed over, and ran up onto the road. The bull stopped short of the fence and stood there snorting and stomping his feet, as if to tell me, "Never come back again!" I took his advice and skipped the last pole in that pasture. By the time Harvey got to the pole, the bull was gone. Harvey said he never saw a bull.

A few weeks later, while we were sitting around the pickup truck having lunch, I once again failed to pay attention to my surroundings.

"Lanny, don't move!" Harvey shouted, as he pointed to the right of me. About five feet from me, a snake lay all coiled and ready to strike if I moved any closer. It was the first rattlesnake we had seen all summer. Harvey grabbed a shovel and walked around to the other side of the pickup. I slowly inched myself away from the snake. There was no need to kill the snake; we just simply packed up and drove off. We watched real close for snakes for the rest of the summer.

"Hey, Dad, is there a special way to iron this graduation gown?"

"Yes, there is. You have to use a damp towel to press the gown to get the wrinkles out. Let me show you how."

It was the night before my high school graduation, and I was getting everything in order for the big day. We had just finished eating. Dad was sober and watching television in the living room when I asked him that question. He got a towel from the kitchen cupboard, ran it under the kitchen faucet, and started to press my graduation gown. I couldn't believe it; I had only seen Dad iron something once before. The discussion that took place, while Dad diligently pressed the wrinkles out of my gown that evening, made for one of the most important days in my life.

"You've had quite a year haven't you, Lanny?"

"I guess so." I wasn't sure what to say. We hadn't had too many heart to heart discussions over the years. I was proud of the year I'd had in school and sports, but didn't want to sound boastful.

Dad looked at me with a warm smile that I hadn't seen very often. "Well, I sure think so! You made the honor roll a couple of times. You had a great year in sports." He put his head down and resumed ironing. "To be honest, Lanny, I never thought you would end up being the young man you are today. I thought for sure you were going to end up behind bars. To this day, I don't understand why you did the things you did when you were a young boy. Why were you such a little devil? Why did you steal stuff? Why did you run away from home all the time?"

"I really don't know why, Dad," I answered with a tone of regret. "I'm just glad you never sent me off to reform school."

"Well, I'm sure glad you changed your ways. If I had sent you off to reform school, your mother would never forgive me. Tomorrow you graduate from high school. Before you know it, August will be here and you'll be off to St. Cloud for college. Who would have thought?"

"I sure hope I make a lot of money doing elevator construction. Mike and I head out on Sunday for New Richland and start work on Monday. We'll be back Friday night for the weekend."

"Keep checking with the railroad," Dad suggested. "You could make some real money if you were to get on with them." He put the gown on a hanger and handed it to me. "Here you are, all pressed and good to go. Congratulations Son. I'm very proud of you! —So is your mother!"

Those words made my heart feel like it was going to explode out of my chest. I had never heard Dad talk about my mother in such a way, like she was always there. Looking back, I guess she was, and always has been.

For three years Dad and I had been attempting to reconcile. We had moved to a house on Eleventh Street during my Junior Year in high school. My senior year Dad gave me free use of the '57 Ford, held no restraints over me, and had cut back on his drinking. I took care of the house, laundry, and made meals. We often watched television together and played cribbage. But, nothing did more to settle the peace between us than that fifteen minute discussion. That night, as I lay in my bed and thought about all that had taken place that evening, I thanked my Lord and my Guardian Angel for a new life. From that day, until his death, Dad and I enjoyed a great relationship.

Lft. Raymond Gamm - Florence Gamm
Rt. Dad – Mom – Ken

Harvey Bud Leroy Lanny Dad Donny

PART THREE
CHOICES

Chapter Eleven
GREAT IDEAS

We can all look back in time and see distinct moments when we made life changing choices. I believe God provides us with the guidance we need. The Holy Spirit and our Guardian Angels try to guide us through our thoughts. But God also gives us a free spirit to make choices. I've either read or heard it said that, "Life is all about choices." I agree! We have choices to make every waking moment of our lives. Most choices have little influence on our life as a whole. However, some choices affect our life forever. Sometimes, we debate a choice in our mind. Something is talking to us trying to get us to distinguish right from wrong, good from bad, safety from hazardous, and need from desire. Sometimes, a mind debate may go on for hours, days, and even years. My choice to quit smoking and stealing when I was in seventh grade was a debate that lasted for a long time, until I finally heard the right message. That choice had a positive impact on my entire teenage years. I would put a few other "choice" moments in my life on that same impact level.

≈

After graduating from high school, I spent the summer working as a carpenter on a grain elevator construction crew and as a Gandy Dancer for the Milwaukee Railroad. In the fall of 1967, I attended St. Cloud State College (SCSC).

Freshmen year in college is a tough time for many students. I was definitely one of those struggling students. By the end of second quarter, I was out of money and failing two classes. On the bright side of things, I had made a pretty good friend who lived two rooms from me in Shoemaker Hall. Lee Carlson, was a wrestler for St. Cloud State, and I was a diver on the swim team. Every evening, we would find ourselves showering in the dorm's community shower, before going down for Athletes' Late Supper. When we would get to the cafeteria, we would join Lee's roommate, Gust Johnson, who would be holding a table for us. We would talk about practices and school, and what was going on in the world in general. Mostly we just watched the female athletes who ate at Shoemaker. When we finished eating, we would usually go back up to Lee's and Gust's room and hang out.

January 23rd, 1968, two days after my nineteenth birthday, was a typical day with one big exception. While we were eating, we observed a news broadcast over the cafeteria television about something called "The Pueblo Incident". The North Koreans had attacked and hijacked the USS Pueblo, a US Naval Ship. The North Koreans claimed that the Pueblo was inside their territorial waters and was spying on them. There was a lot of tension remaining from the Korean Conflict coupled with the Vietnam War. I didn't think much about the whole incident. Korea and Vietnam were a long way away from St. Cloud State. I was more concerned with how I was going to pay for third quarter's tuition and how to pass the history class I was failing.

When we got back to our dorm rooms, Lee and Gust invited me in to watch the news. I told them I wasn't interested, and that I had a history final to study for.

"This is history in the making," Gust responded.

"If I don't study for my test tomorrow, I'll be history! I'll see you later."

I went to my room and spent the next half hour trying to study "1865 to The Present". It was hopeless. There was just too much to cram for, and I was terrible at Blue Book Exams. I was going to fail history class no matter how much I studied. I made a life altering choice. I went back to Lee and Gust's room.

"Hey Lanny, we've got a great idea!" Lee exclaimed as I entered their room.

"What's that?"

Gust seemed all pumped, "The Marines are offering a two year enlistment so we're going down to the recruiter's office tomorrow to check it out. Do you want to come along?"

"I don't know. I've never thought about enlisting— the Marines?"

Lee added, "The Army has a three year enlistment. The Navy and Air Force are both four year enlistments. If we get full GI benefits for a two year enlistment, it would be worth it."

"We're just going to check it out," Gust assured me. "Come along and check it out for yourself."

"I guess it won't hurt to go and see what they have to offer," I said reluctantly.

We hung out for the rest of the evening listening to the news about the Pueblo and the casualty reports from Vietnam. I went back to my room with an uneasy feeling in the pit of my stomach. Now I was really confused. I spent the night thinking about what I was going to do with my life? I didn't even know why I was going to college. I had no clue as to what I was going to major in. Should I go back to doing construction or working on the railroad? I had been offered good jobs with both companies. Would they take me back? If I enlisted in the Marines for two years, would I be volunteering for Vietnam?

The Marine Recruiter's office was pretty inspiring. "A Few Good Men" was plastered everywhere along with "Semper Fidelis". A sergeant in Dress Blues was quick to greet us at the door.

"So, you guys think you've got what it takes to be a Marine?"

"We're just here to check things out," Gust responded.

"Ya'll just look around. If ya'll got questions just, ask." The recruiter sounded like he was from another country.

Lee quickly asked, "What can you tell us about your two year enlistment?"

"We just started the program last week to build up numbers of recruits."

"Will we get all the GI benefits when we get out?" Lee added.

"Ya'll be able to go to school, buy a house, and get medical treatment through the GI Bill."

"Will the government pay for all of my schooling?" I asked.

"No. But they pay for a pretty big chunk of it," the recruiter answered. "Ya'll get the same benefits whether you serve two years or four. The only requirement is that you receive an honorable discharge from the Marine Corps."

We continued to look around at all the posters and information. The idea of the government paying for my schooling was really inviting to me. I didn't know where I was going to get my next quarter's tuition. Dad had already signed for one student deferred loan with the bank and I knew he wouldn't sign for another one if I was failing a class.

The recruiter broke the silence, "We have another enlistment program that ya'll might be interested in called the 'Buddy System'. This program guarantees that you and your buddy will stay together throughout basic training. I could get the three of ya'll in under the program."

"I always figured I'd serve my country sometime. I guess now is as good a time as any. It doesn't look like we're going to be out of Vietnam anytime soon. So, by enlisting under this program I think we're pretty much volunteering for Vietnam," Lee surmised.

"Let's do it, Lee!" Gust exploded. "Being together through basic will help a lot."

Hearing their reactions helped me make my choice to enlist. I think Lee and Gust have always felt that they pressured me into enlisting with them that day, but I pretty much made my choice based on the potential of the GI Bill. The "Buddy System" made the choice a lot easier. It was a choice that set the mold for the rest of my life.

"Why the Marine Corps? They're the front lines!" Dad went on and on. "You know you're going to Vietnam by enlisting for just two years. They're going to train you and send you over there to get shot or blown up."

"I know. But I believe that if I'm meant to make it back, I will. I've given this a lot of thought and it's what I want to do. I go for my induction physical in the Cities tomorrow."

For the next few weeks, I worked for Dad at the grain elevator warehouse. It was good to work with Dad, and as time passed he got used to the idea of me joining the Marines. Once I heard him proudly say to a customer, "He's my son. He's going to Marine Corps Boot Camp next week."

Chapter Twelve
WELCOME TO VIETNAM

"All right you bloody maggots, you've got fifteen seconds to get your asses out onto the blacktop and find a set of yellow footprints to stand on!" The Marine went to each bus and repeated the order.

Everyone on the bus grabbed his duffle bag and made a mad rush for the door and attempted to accomplish what the Marine at the front of the bus had told us to do. We were like a heard of cattle fighting to get to the water hole. Lee and Gust had been right next to me on the bus. Now I had no clue as to where they were among the one hundred plus recruits scrambling to find a set of prints. I thought to myself, as I stood on my yellow footprints, "What have I gotten myself into?"

"Welcome to the San Diego Marine Corps Recruit Deport! I'm sergeant Barera! I'll be one of your drill instructors during your little stay here! I'll be replacing your mama and papa! I'll correct all the mistakes they made raising you and making you the puny maggots you are! I'll turn you into a lean, mean, fighting machine! Do you understand?!" I didn't think he was ever going to quit barking.

Half of us made a feeble attempt to answer the sergeant with, "Yes, Sir!"

"What is your problem maggot? Didn't your mommy teach you how to answer a question?" The sergeant was screaming at a recruit with their faces two inches apart. "When you're asked a question, you answer with 'Sir, Yes, Sir, or Sir, No, Sir!' Do you understand maggot?!"

"Sir, Yes, Sir," the recruit squeaked.

"I can't hear you!" barked the drill instructor again with his face so close it looked like he was yelling down the recruit's throat.

"Sir, Yes, Sir!" This time the recruit barked back.

For the next twelve weeks, my life was full of drill instructors barking out orders, physical training, marching, and class work. I decided early that I would treat boot camp like one big football practice. My high school football coaches would have made good drill instructors. I was pretty comfortable with all aspects of boot camp, except for all the marching. We marched from sunrise to sundown. If we weren't marching to wherever we went, we were jogging. But I knew it was an important tool for developing pride, unity, conditioning, and discipline. I knew millions of recruits had made it through before me, and I would make it too.

I was surprised at how academic the Marine Corps was. We were given Marine Corps Handbooks to study. We would attend two or three lectures and demonstrations every day. Each platoon competed with all the other platoons in the company for the achievement ribbon for each component of training. The Academic Ribbon was the most coveted by drill instructors because it brought the most points toward being the Company Honor Platoon at graduation.

One warm Sunday morning, while we were sitting and cleaning our rifles outside our barracks, an order rang through the air, "Private Saumer report to the Duty Hut!"

Up until now, I hadn't been singled out for anything. I was all flustered. My rifle was in pieces on the ground, so I tried frantically to reassemble it.

"Saumer, get your ass to the Duty Hut, Now!" Sergeant Barera Roared.

"Jesus, Lanny, what the hell have you done?" Lee asked with a look of real concern. "I'll look after your rifle."

I hustled to the Duty Hut. "Sir, Private Saumer, reporting to the Duty Hut Sir!"

"Private Saumer, you have to be the slowest maggot in the platoon. Didn't you play football in high school?"

"Sir, Yes, Sir!"

"You must have had a horse-shit team!"

"Sir, Yes, Sir!" The truth was we were rated number one in the state until we lost our final game of the season by one point. But, I was so scared I was willing to agree to anything the drill instructor said.

"It says here that you have had a couple of years of Spanish classes."

"Sir, Yes, Sir!" I had taken Spanish in ninth and tenth grade in high school.

"Why did you drop out of college?"

"Sir, to get the 'GI Bill,' Sir!"

"Well, you'll have to get your ass back from Vietnam first." Sergeant Barera wasn't shouting anymore. He was actually talking to me in a civil tone.

"I'm going to give you an opportunity to put your Spanish lessons to work. I've got six Mexican-American recruits in this platoon. I'm going to make you a Squad Leader and these six "Wet-Backs" will be in your squad. They can't read or speak much English. Your number one job will be to make sure they all graduate. No one is to know that you are helping them! Do you understand, Private?"

"Sir, Yes, Sir!"

I had been given the first teaching assignment of my life. I worked with those six recruits for eleven weeks of boot camp. I had nothing to work with, not even a Spanish-English Dictionary, only the Marine Corps Handbook. We struggled through it all, and in the end, everyone did pass. They probably ended up teaching me as much as I did them. Because of their success, I was promoted to "Private First Class" (PFC) and awarded the distinction of being the "Platoon Honor Man" at graduation. They were the only explanation for me getting such a distinction because I never excelled at any component of training. But I was a good squad leader. Once we graduated boot camp, I never saw any of them again. I do not know how many of them passed the "ultimate test" and returned from Vietnam.

Lee had been given a special assignment in boot camp also. Lee excelled at all the physical fitness components of our training. I think he may have even made a buck or two doing push-ups in the barracks at night. It was no surprise when he was put in charge of the physical fitness squad. Any recruit who was struggling with the fitness portion of our training was put in Lee's squad for extra training and conditioning. Lee was under extra pressure because our friend Gust was put in the fitness squad. Everyone made it through fine and Lee was promoted to PFC for the graduation ceremony.

Gust ended up excelling on the rifle range, outshooting both Lee and me, and qualifying "Expert".

We were given our Military Occupational Specialty (MOS) on graduation day. Lee and I were both assigned infantry, and Gust was assigned communications. Those assignments dictated our next line of training. That meant we would be split up. Lee and I were sent to Basic Infantry Training School (BITS), but with different companies. Gust was sent to Communications School. So much for the recruiter's "Buddy Plan". I never saw Gust again while in the Corps. I ran into Lee a couple of times in BITS and one time in Vietnam. All we could do was pray for one another.

While in BITS a Marine from boot camp named Bob Hulsey and I became better friends. Bob was older than the rest of us. He was 26, married and had a son. Most of us were 18 or 19. Bob was from Missouri and had an accent like I had never heard before. In some ways, he reminded me a lot of my brother— same age, same size, and same personality.

The first weekend we were given furlough, Bob and I decided to go to Disneyland instead of going south of the border into Mexico. As we were leaving the barrack, another Marine, Bill, asked if he could join us. So, the three of us set out for a week-end that would have an impact on the rest of my life.

We checked into a cheap motel a couple of blocks from Disneyland. I remember being quite excited for my first trip to the world famous amusement park. We probably looked like three stud Marines strutting around the park like proud peacocks. It wasn't long before some young girls hustled us into letting them be our dates for the evening. It was pretty much a win-win situation. The girls got free rides and snacks. We got to ride with a pretty girl instead of each other. Just looking around the park you could see this was a common practice. When the evening was done, the girls went their way and we went ours. The evening had been a blast!

The next morning we went to a Pancake House restaurant for breakfast. I ordered a Blueberry Belgian Waffle. I had never had one before in my life. When we were about halfway through our breakfasts, a man across the aisle interrupted us.

"Is this your first furlough?" he asked.

"Yes, Sir," Hulsey replied.

"Did you go to Disneyland last night?" The man inquired with a friendly tone.

"We sure did. What a 'fascnaten' place!" Hulsey's Missouri accent was coming through.

The man introduced himself and his wife as Bob and Mary Lou Tilt. He told us they were both teachers and lived in Huntington Beach. Bob was also a retired Air Force Staff-Sergeant. We continued to visit for quite some time. As we were getting ready to leave, Bob Tilt made a strange proposal. "How would you guys like to have a nice comfortable place to go for your weekend furloughs?"

"What do you mean?" I inquired.

Mary Tilt interjected, "We have a tradition of offering our home as a retreat for one or two Marines during their training. We would love to have the three of you come. We have a pool and a spare room. We also have three young daughters, but they're used to having Marines around. They say it's like having big brothers. Here is our phone number. If you're interested, give us a call and we'll pick you up at the bus depot."

I reached for the card and said, "Thank you for such a generous offer."

As I took the card from Mary Lou's hand she gave me a hug and whispered in my ear, "God bless you, Lanny!" I'll never forget the warmth I felt at that moment!

As they were getting into their car, Mary Lou repeated, this time out loud, "God bless you, Boys!" Then they drove off.

We couldn't believe it. We had only known these people for an hour or so, and now they had offered us their home for retreat. Were they some California weirdoes? Or, were they just some nice people? Would we ever see them again?

The week that followed that furlough was pure hell. We all looked forward to the weekend break from marching and eating dust all day. There weren't too many left in the barracks when I saw Hulsey sitting on his footlocker.

As I approached him, he looked up and asked me, "You got that card those kind people gave us last week?"

I took the card out of my wallet and handed it to him. "Are you really going to call them?" I asked.

"I'm a married man, Lanny. I can't go around trying to get into some young girl's panties."

Hulsey was my best friend in BITS so I replied, "Let's do it!"

We spent the rest of our training furloughs at the Tilts' home. We hung around the pool, went on picnics, and puttered around the house. (Hulsey was a carpenter by trade). We became family. The oldest girl, Mary Ann (Ann), became a very close friend and wrote me almost every day while I was in Vietnam. The two younger girls, Cathy and Jane, were like little sisters. The entire Tilt family has remained dear friends with both Bob Hulsey and me for forty years. This past year, 2008,

Bob Tilt finally retired from teaching. Mary Lou had retired a couple of years ago. Over the 57 years of their marriage, Bob and Mary Lou Tilt have given refuge to some thirty Marines. Some of those Marines went to California this past summer for Bob's retirement party. Hulsey was one of those Marines. I was unable to attend due to my medical condition at the time.

Jumping out of a chopper twenty feet off the ground, with bullets zinging through the air leaves a lasting impression; such was my welcome to Vietnam, on October 3rd, 1968. I arrived on the 2nd and was assigned to Hotel Company 2-9 out of Quang Tri. The company was out in the bush, so I had to be choppered out to join them. When we arrived, the company was under fire. The chopper couldn't land and we had to jump out, hit the ground, roll, get up, get our bearings, and run for cover. As it turned out, the place in Vietnam I was jumping into was known as Khe Sanh. Khe Sanh had been a major battle sight during the TET Offensive, which had ended a couple of weeks earlier. My Guardian Angel was already at work and had gotten me through my first real firefight.

I spent four months marching through the jungles of the DMZ. We rarely saw much; Charlie would be long gone by the time we got there. I had gotten word about a special program unit called CAP (Combined Action Program). The program involved working with Vietnamese villagers. CAP had gotten a lot of mixed reviews in the field. Sometimes you heard about how great it was. You just sat around some village eating and drinking. Other rumors told of a life filled with constant danger and conflict with the Viet-Cong. What I did know was that you worked as a small group of Marines providing security for a small Vietnamese village. Also, before you could become a CAP Marine, you had to go to two weeks of intense training in Da Nang. By the end of December, I decided to put in for it and wait to see if I got the transfer.

Every couple of weeks we would get to go to the rear, let our guard down, and relax. One such weekend came after sitting guard for an Arvin Artillery base. We were able to get anything we wanted on that Arvin base. Before we left, I purchased two quarts of 45 Brand Whiskey. That night, January 21, 1969, my buddy and I celebrated my 20th birthday with everyone's blessing. Jeff and I sat on a mound of dirt and downed a quart of that 45 Brand Whiskey. We proceeded to take a little hike down the road to see what else was going on. We came upon a group sitting around a fire smoking weed. I had never tried weed before, and didn't like it being smoked in the bush, but since we were due to remain in the rear for a couple of days, I figured I'd give it a try. Jeff and I had already downed a quart of whiskey so what could a couple of weeds do? After a few passes of the weed, Jeff and I felt like we would rather go back to the mound and drink some more. I can't say that either choice was too bright, but we weren't in any condition to know better. Jeff went to his tent and brought back a second bottle of 45 Brand Whiskey. (It is important to interject here that until this moment in my life, I had never been intoxicated.) Jeff and I managed to finish off that second bottle by sharing it with the likes of many others, such as the Gunny and the Lieutenant. Eventually a cry came from the officer's tent telling everyone to get some shut-eye.

My platoon's tent was just below the mound of dirt on which we had been celebrating. I easily found my way to my backpack and supplies. I pulled out my rubber mattress and started blowing it up. I hadn't blown very long before I became extremely nauseous. I darted out the end of the tent and looked frantically for somewhere to vomit. I tripped over some guide ropes and ended up in another tent, and I let it fly.

"Who in the hell is that puking all over my gear?!" roared a voice from the officer's tent.

"Sir, Lance Corporal Saumer, Sir. I've had too much to drink for my birthday, Sir!"

"Well, happy birthday Marine! Now get your puny ass out of my tent!"

I managed to crawl back to my mattress. I didn't bother blowing it up. I just went to sleep. In what appeared to be hardly any time at all, but had actually been several hours, I felt someone kicking my feet and yelling. "Get your sorry assess up! We have to be back out in the bush by 0700. We will be getting air lifted out. Be on the road in fifteen!"

My first hangover was defeated by a two mile march in full gear to the chopper, only to suffer air sickness all the way out to the bush. We put down close to the Border of Laos on the Ho Chi Minh Trail. There had obviously been a lot of recent traffic by the Viet Cong. Our job was to interrupt the human train of weapons and bodies being transported up and down the border. It was here that I saw my first dead Vietnamese body. While on patrol, we came across a dead North Vietnamese Officer. The man had been dead several days. Checking his belongings revealed a list of names and a map, as well as some personal pictures of his family. He didn't seem much different from the rest of us. He had probably gotten drunk on his birthday, too.

A couple of days later, I was called to the Captain's Tent. "Saumer, get you gear together, you lucky S.O.B., you're being transferred to CAP! There'll be a chopper here to take you to Da Nang in fifteen."

CAP School was indeed intense. We studied the Vietnamese language, their culture, and their government. We learned how to read maps and call in artillery and air strikes. We learned how to interrogate a prisoner. I remember being on watch at school during the TET on January 30th, 1969. (TET is the Vietnamese New Year.) Everyone was all tensed up because of what had happened the year before. I heard a few rat-tat-tats and that was it. Most nights were spent at the NCO (Non-Commissioned Officers) lounge drinking beer and eating ice cream. It was a good two weeks of schooling, but I was ready to get out to my unit.

I was assigned the 1st Combined Action Group out of Chu Lai Vietnam, about 20 miles south of Da Nang. From Chu Lai, I was sent out to a small peninsula called Ahn Hi to join my platoon 1-4-3. As we flew low over the villages, I could see the vast difference from being up North. We could see people in rice patties and walking the roads everywhere. Those people would have been blown away in the North.

When I arrived in the middle of the day, my group was waiting for me so they could move out. My arrival brought the unit's number to eleven— ten Marines and one future Corpsman. Sergeant Anderson was the NCO in command. There were a couple of Corporals and a couple of other Lance Corporals along with me and then a few PFCs. We didn't have a Corpsman. We were a small group, but we were expected to do it all.

Our job was to see that the peninsula was secure of any Viet-Cong. Ahn Hi had once been a "rest and relaxation"(R&R) get away for the Viet-Cong. The US bombed the peninsula to drive the Viet-Cong out, but in the process they also drove out all the villagers. Once we had secured the peninsula, our job would be to resettle the village refugees and provide them security. Each day a group of four would go on a search mission. During our searches we would come across a few hide-a-ways. We would call for a chopper to take them to the Quang Nai Refugee Camp.

One day was memorable. It was going to be Al's last mission because he only had three days left in Nam. Bill had a little over a week left and was talking about his marriage and all the plans he had stateside. The short-timers hadn't been gone long when we heard a loud explosion come from their direction. Sgt. Anderson tried to make contact with them but couldn't get an answer. We all got our gear on and headed out. What we saw when we got to the sight was beyond imagination. Al was alive, but with both of his legs gone. He looked at me and said, "Help me, Lanny."

While Sgt Anderson attended to Al, I assessed the rest of the situation. I saw where the radio pack had been set on a booby-trapped rock. The compression coming out from under the rock caused Al's legs to be blown away. There was a trench running about fifteen feet along the ground to Bill's body. When we rolled him over, we discovered that a piece of shrapnel had embedded in his head. The trench was from Bill trying to drive the pain from his head. I remember being in a state of shock on the verge of laughing. The chopper came and we loaded up our dear friends and said good bye. I lowered my head and acknowledged that here only by the Grace of God and my Guardian Angel stood I.

We continued our search missions for a few more days. We finally got an order to find a good spot to resettle the village refugees. We had found a place but we were far from ready for the refugees. Nonetheless, we were ordered to go get them from the other side of the peninsula and walk them across to our area. A feat we thought was very dangerous with booby-traps and snipers. We carried out the mission without flaw. The refugees got to the beach happy as larks and quickly set up camp. The CAP platoon went to the top of the hill alongside the village. A road had been plowed to the top of the hill, and the top of the hill was leveled. The message seemed plain enough; we were to build our compound at the top of the hill. This all looked too convenient for my peace of mind. Because I was scheduled for night patrol, I took another Marine, Joe, with me and we cut a path down the opposite side of the hill. Everyone got their tent pitched and a two man fox hole dug. We spent a little time trying to clear fields of fire but the brush was just too thick. Eventually, nighttime came, and it was time to go out on night patrol. Joe and I, along with two Vietnamese Popular Forces, who were like our national guard, headed down the plowed trail through the village and back down the road from where we had come with the refugees earlier in the day. If Charlie had been watching us all day, I wanted him to think we would return the same way. When our four hour watch was up, we headed back to our compound. I lead the way by taking us up the back trail we had made earlier. Sgt Anderson was expecting us when we got to the top of the hill. I reported to him that all was quiet down below.

Things didn't remain quiet for long. Within fifteen minutes of our return, all hell broke loose. I had just lain down in my tent for the night. BOOM! A huge explosion sounded like it was inside our compound. Whistles were blowing! The rat-tat-tats of rifles were going off all around. I slipped down into my fox hole with my rifle and some hand grenades. Bob was already in the hole. "Are you OK Bob?"

"I'm fine. We have VC coming through the line everywhere. I think they got Bell with the first blast on the fifty. "

Bob had no sooner said that, when I saw an image big as life coming over the bank. I raised my rifle without a thought and squeezed off half a dozen rounds. I could see the tracer rounds going right through him. Sgt Anderson had called in for some artillery support. An Army compound on the other side of the bay was illuminating the sky. As quickly as things started, it also stopped. We hung tight until day break.

At Sgt's orders we were to check out the fire lanes in front of our holes. I checked mine expecting to fine a dead body. There was nothing, only the drag marks. Upon further investigation we discovered that our night patrol team had been set up to be ambushed when we returned. Our little back door maneuver saved four lives. Nonetheless, we did lose CPL Bell and the fifty caliber machine gun.

When Bob and I returned to our tent, we were in for another surprise. About six inches from where my head had been was a dead "potato smasher" (a German hand grenade). There by the Grace of God and my Guardian Angel stood I. The next day we moved our camp down along the beach until the village people cleared all the brush away around the hill.

≈

I believe that sometimes a Guardian Angel protects more than just the person to whom they are assigned. Sometimes they need to protect the innocent people who are around when their subject makes a blundering mistake. Several days after being overrun on the hill, we were setting up security for the night. I would set off several preliminary mortar shots with our M-80 Mortar. As we were doing this, one of the mortar rounds didn't sound right. This usually meant that it would be a short round. In this case a short round meant it would land in the village. BOOM! Sure enough the blast was near the village well, of all places.

We went running to the well. People were screaming. I ran back to the compound tent and called in a medevac. I ran back to the well. One child was wounded and one woman crying hysterically. The chopper came and the two victims were evacuated. I expressed an apology to the village. They already knew what had happened and accepted it as a necessary evil. Two days later I was promoted to Corporal for handling of the situation.

The villagers eventually cleared the hill and we moved the compound back up onto the hill. Sgt. Anderson had completed his tour of duty; leaving CPL Bob and me in dual command of the platoon. We worked things out so that Bob was in charge of the compound and I was in charge of maneuvers and the village. We had things pretty nice. We had sandbagged bunkers, sandbagged foxholes, a sandbagged communications bunker, and sandbagged mortar holes and gun holes. We had concertina wire all around the compound. Very little action would occur around the compound. Once in a while we would take on some sniper fire while on patrol.

One day, I was taking some villagers across the peninsula to the village on the other side. We were well on our way when we stopped to give a situation report. As I grabbed hold of the radio phone we heard a rat-tat-tat. We all dove for the bomb crater along side the road. While I was flying through the air, I felt a huge thump against my hip. I figured it was the radioman kicking me as we dove into the crater together. As we lay in the crater we kept getting sniper fire. I reported back to the main office and gave them our situation. They sent out an air strike in about two minutes. End of sniper fire.

When the smoke had all gone, we got up from the crater. All the Vietnamese Popular Forces started laughing at me and pointing at my hip and chanted, "Sam, Charlie no can cockadow!" I understood what they were saying but didn't understand why. They were saying that Charlie couldn't kill me. (Sam was their nickname for me). But why were they saying that? I looked down at where they were pointing. I untied my magazine holder from around my hips. There, lodged in one of my magazines was an AK-47 round. All I suffered was a bruised hip. There by the Grace of God and my Guardian Angel stood I.

There were other fire fights, ambushes, and compound invasions. I went through them all knowing that God and my Guardian Angel were going to get me back home again. I never became careless but always listened, in my mind, to the Holy Spirit helping me to make the right choice and I counted on my guardian angel to protect me and those with me.

≈

I did a lot of teaching while I was stationed with CAP-143. It was our job to teach Popular Forces, which were local young men in the village who had an older brother in the regular Army. This was a bit ironic because some of these young men were also Viet Cong. Nevertheless, it was our job to teach them how to run patrols, set up security, set up an ambush, and how to use various weapons.

We were also required to do a fair amount of civic service. I chose to work with the Corpsman in the medical clinic two mornings each week. The first building the villagers built was a school. I was excited about that and offered a lot of my time and effort toward the building and running of the school. The school also served as the town hall and barber shop.

It was the second time the Marine Corps had put me in a teaching situation.

Chapter Thirteen
BOAT RIDE

On September 4th, 1969 I boarded the USS Iwo Jima Helicopter Carrier. I was being sent home as one of President Nixon's big troop withdrawals. Hell, I was due to come home anyhow. Nevertheless, they messed with me in Guam. They confiscated my m16 magazine that had stopped the AK 47 round from taking my right leg. They didn't care about my story.

I had never been on a ship before. It was incredible! The chopper carrier was a floating city. The crew numbered around a thousand. Three Thousand Marines were being shipped home on this one huge ship.

The thirty day trip on ship allowed me to easily quit smoking. I was standing on the aft of the ship's deck when I decided to quit. It was neat to see the water turn over and over until it disappeared as the ship's huge propellers moved the ship along. I enjoyed the calming effect and made it a daily ritual to go back there to watch the water and have a cigarette. I didn't suffer any sea-sickness, but one day I just didn't want to be a cigarette smoker any more. I had been down that route once before in my life and didn't like what it had gotten me.

It was strange that among three thousand Marines I didn't know anyone. This was pretty much the same situation for everyone. It didn't take long before I linked up with a couple of guys and hung around together. Every night was movie night. Imagine a couple thousand bodies crammed into a hanger to watch a movie. Most of us hadn't seen a movie for over a year, so we didn't care about a little body odor. However, by the end of the trip I couldn't stand a person's body odor; it made me nauseous and it still does today.

One of my favorite things to do on the ship was to watch the sun rise and set. It really is one of nature's masterpieces. One night, while enjoying the sunset, I thought a lot about what I was going to do when I got out of the Marine Corps in a few days. I knew I was going to go back to school at St. Cloud State. I thought about the Mexicans I taught in boot camp. I had helped the villagers build their school and taught their children some simple English. I had taught the Popular Forces. The message seemed pretty clear. I should become a teacher. I thought about my high school days and what subjects I liked. I was just an average student making the B Honor Roll a couple of times. Without a doubt my favorite class was Geometry. I loved figuring things out in geometry class. I still have my high school geometry notebook with all my beautifully written proofs. You can bet your last dollar that those proofs have come in handy many times in my life. I decided on the deck of the USS Iwo Jima, while watching a beautiful sunset, that I would become a math teacher.

We were lucky in that we never had one storm while we were at sea. As a result, we made it stateside a full day ahead of schedule. That meant we had an extra day of furlough after we got our medical discharge. I went with two other guys across the border to Tijuana. I had heard horror stories about Tijuana, but I was a year older and a salty Marine so I agreed to go. We hired a limo driver to take care of us and he did a real good job. We had a great time! I purchased some very nice art pieces for family members and Onyx chess set for myself.

On the second day of our furlough, I called Bob and Mary Tilt. They picked me up and took me to their home for two days. We had a wonderful visit. They told me how Bob Hulsey had been home for some time due to a combat medical discharge. We gave him a call and had a great visit even though he wasn't doing too well. Hulsey was divorced and had lost his son in a car accident. After our phone call to Bob Hulsey, the Tilts shared some other disheartening news. Bill Wiemer, the third Marine who had spent some time at the Tilts with Bob and me, had been killed in action a few of months earlier.

As cold as it may seem, I could not find it in me to be overly sad. I was too elated to be safe and sound at home with friends. No booby traps to worry about, no incoming to seek cover from, and no medevacs to arrange. We went for a swim in the pool and ate some barbeque. I was a very lucky man to have the Tilts to come home to. They understood where I had been, what I had seen, and knew what I needed.

As the night progressed, the inevitable happened. Ann asked me to go for a walk down to the wharf. I consented with a terrible fear in the back of my mind. Ann was greatly responsible for me making it back from Vietnam mentally sane. Her letters gave me purpose every day. She had shared so much with me in her letters. I knew she was hoping that our relationship would develop into something more than pen-pals. Ann wasted no time placing her arm in mine as we walked down the sidewalk. I must confess, it was a very good feeling, but one I wasn't sure I was ready for. As we walked, Ann chattered on about the year she was having in high school. She was a senior and hoped to go on to medical school next year. I told her that I had decided to go back to St. Cloud State and pursue a teaching degree in math. She mentioned that California had great teacher colleges.

We spent the night enjoying the moment. We laughed and told stories, walked barefoot in the sandy beach, and chased each other. It felt so good to be free! Ann was so sweet and beautiful! When we returned to the house we stopped before going inside. I took Ann in my arms and kissed her. A mistake I would correct at another time. The next day the Tilts took me to the airport to catch my flight home to Minneapolis where my brother, Ken, picked me up to take me home.

An Hai Village—1969

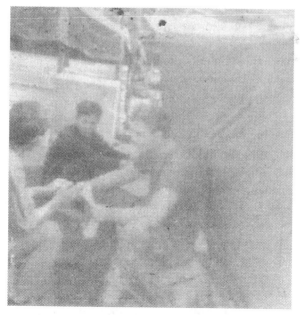

Planning with Village Chief and PF-seargent

An Hai Village Students — 1969

Passing out school supplies — 1969

PART FOUR
FAMILY TIES

Chapter Fourteen

COLLEGE DAYS

*L*ee Carlson had made it home a couple of weeks before me. Gust Johnson was still in Vietnam. I called Lee to check on things. His plans were to return to school second quarter as well. He was delivering milk for his dad at the Almalund Dairy. I agreed to go to St. Cloud, find us an apartment, and then, drive over to Almalund to see him and his folks.

It seems that there are only a few people who you meet in this world whose personalities leave a lasting imprint in your mind. Arlene and Paul Carlson were such people. Paul was retired from the US Air Force and was working at the local creamery. Lee often talked about all the places he had lived while his dad was in the service. Paul was set in his ways and had little hope for the new generation. Arlene worked at the local post office and was as pure as fresh fallen snow. I remember Lee sharing some words of advice his mother gave him one evening as he was going out for a date. "Don't create a life of regrets for a moment of pleasure." Lee was a lucky man to have had such a wise mother. I always thought my mother would have given me that same advice.

The apartment I found for Lee and me to make our great return to college life ended up to be quite a bust. It was a basement apartment all the way across town about four miles from campus. Our roommate, Les, was an ex-convict out on probation. He drank and smoked constantly. About the only thing I remember about that place is the night I had to write a big brother letter to Ann Tilt. I told her she was a beautiful person and that I loved her for all she had done for me, but only like a big brother. We have maintained that brother – sister relationship over the years through my ongoing friendship with her parents.

"Hey Saumer, where have you been?" came a voice from behind me, as I was walking from Hallenbeck Hall to Stewart Hall. "I haven't seen you on campus for a long time. Where have you been hiding?"

"I've been studying on the other side of the world," I told Jerry, a former classmate. I explained to him that I had enlisted in the Marines, done a tour of duty in Vietnam, and was back in college on the 'GI Bill'. His questions brought with them an awakening reality for me. What had seemed forever for me, had really only been a short period of time. Most of the faces on campus were the same. Everyone was hustling from class to class. Life hadn't changed here at all. That realization brought with it a bit of concern because I knew I had changed a lot. There was a lot of defiance on campuses throughout the country towards the war in Vietnam. How much hassle would I get when people learned where I had been? As it turned out, I never got hassled at all. For the most part, everyone respected my service, whether they agreed with the war or not. I was split as to how I felt about the war, so I was always open to discussion.

My attempt to major in Math in pursuit of a teaching degree didn't go so well. That first quarter back at school, I figured I would take a good math refresher course. College Algebra and Trigonometry would be the key to open my door to the math world of teaching. I was doing very well in the class until the first exam. I committed a cardinal sin of test taking. I spent too much time on the first problem without looking through the entire test first and then doing the problems I knew best. As a result, I had several easy problems left on the test when time ran out. I ended up failing the exam so miserably that it took getting mostly "A's" the rest of the quarter for me to get a "C" for the course.

As fate would have it, while I was struggling in my math class, I was also taking a General Biology class. I couldn't wait to get to class on Biology day. Dr. Peck was just incredible. He made the class come alive as he would imitate different animal behaviors in front of the auditorium class. For the first time in my life, I got an "A" in a Biology class. I had a chance to take another class with Dr. Peck the next quarter. All the meaningful lab activities and the teacher enthusiasm sold me on declaring Biology as my Major and Physical Education as my Minor courses of study. I guess I have Dr. Peck to thank for a thirty-two year career teaching Middle School Science. Lee was so impressed with my commitment that he decided to go the same route and major in Biology and minor in Physical Education.

After Winter Quarter, Lee and I moved to an apartment nearer to campus. Except for me, 1520 Michigan Avenue would be our address for the rest of our college years. Gust would eventually join us, as well as a wrestling friend of Lee's from New York, Billy Raffloer. With Lee, Gust, and me on the GI Bill, we had it pretty nice. Lee and Billy wrestled for St. Cloud State and I was a diver on the college swim team. I eventually got a part time job at a granite company making fireplace mantles and hearths. Classes were interesting, parties were often, girls were plenty, and life was simply good.

During this period of time I took up the guitar. As part of my nature, I became obsessive about learning and playing. At times I think I almost drove Lee, Gust, and Billy nuts. I would practice for hours. The guys were so kind and never complained; I know at times it was bad. Eventually I became somewhat proficient at playing the guitar, as well as writing and singing songs. The following is the first song I wrote on January 2, 1971:

I wake up in the morning and the sun shines down on me.
I thank the Lord for another day and for being free.
Then I realize what a lucky man am I, to live in this country— for
    which so many men have died.
Then I go on my way, just like any other day, and I forget about all
    those men who have died.

Then I come home at night, and I turn on the tube, only to hear
all that's not right.

I hear about all the men that died today and how the young ones
have gone astray.

Then I climb into my bed, and I grab that book I've seldom read.

And I ask the Lord why thy must die.

Why oh why, must so many men have to die?

Then I wake up in the morning, and the sun shines down on me.

I thank the Lord for another day and for being free.

Then I realize what a lucky man am I, to live in this country—for
which so many men have died.

Christmas of 1971 and Easter of 1972 may very well have been the
ultimate in my Guardian Angel's life interventions. Aunt Phyl invited Dad
and me to join her and Uncle Bud for Christmas. My cousin, Robyn, whose
husband Larry (the same Larry I grew up with on 6ᵗʰ Street) was stationed
in Vietnam, was living with her folks in Albert Lea, Minnesota.

One evening during our Christmas visit, we were playing cards.
Joining the family for cards was Robyn's friend. As we played cards I
became more and more impressed by Robyn's friend, Karen Chance.
She was a very pretty girl with a lot of spunk who had graduated
from high school the year before and now worked with Robyn at the
Montgomery Ward store in Albert Lea. While we were playing "Spite
and Malice," I noticed her give my dad an elbow when he would play a
card that would hurt her hand. I couldn't help but respect her for that.
Karen sure knew how to make people have fun.

"Lanny, do you know how to play cribbage?" Karen asked me after
we were done playing Spite and Malice.

"Sure," I answered.

"Well, let's play then," she suggested. "Bud and Phyl have a really
neat board."

While we were playing our second or third game, Karen asked, "Would you like to go with Robyn and me to the Ward's Christmas party tomorrow night?"

I was rather surprised that she would ask me to a party after only a few hours of playing cards. I figured she was just being nice to her friend's cousin, so I said, "Yes."

That night, I asked Robyn to tell me a little about this Karen. I learned that she had once been my cousin, Brian's, girlfriend in high school. She was a loving and free spirited girl. Karen was giving her a lot of love and support while Larry was in Vietnam. Robyn told me Karen would be an easy person for me to talk to about anything.

The next evening, as we pulled up behind an orange-yellow Ford Pinto, Karen come flying out from a gray house to the right. Her long brunette hair and burgundy pant suit were flowing through the air as she approached the car.

"I think she's a little excited!" Robyn laughed.

Karen jumped into the car and never quit talking until we got to the party. I was quite amused.

The party was going very nicely until I managed to spill half a pitcher of coffee over the arm of one of Karen's friends. To save me from prolonged embarrassment, Karen grabbed my elbow and dragged me out onto the dance floor. We enjoyed a couple of dances together.

After the party, we went to one of Karen's friend's home to hang out. Karen and I sat by the fireplace and visited.

The next day, Dad and I left early in the morning because I had to drive him home to Montevideo, and then, drive to St. Cloud; a total of about seven hours of driving. Dad asked me how the party had gone. I told him it went okay.

I was glad to get back to school. We had a dozen swim meets ahead of us before Spring Break, Biology classes were getting more intense and more interesting, there were parties to go to, and a lot of guitar playing. I dated four girls between Christmas and Spring Break but never found any of them very interesting. Some of those dates turned out to be outright awkward. I know Lee remembers coming home early from a wrestling tournament one night, only to find me and one of his ex-girlfriends together on the sofa. We still laugh about that.

When Spring Break came, my Guardian Angel took complete control. I was half way to Montevideo when an idea popped into my head. I would ask Dad to go with me back to Albert Lea for Easter. Dad had no interest in making the long trip but wished me well in my pursuit.

Bud and Phyl weren't completely surprised when they saw me pull into their driveway shortly before noon. "What brings you back to Albert Lea?" asked Phyl. "It wouldn't have anything with that brunette bitch across town would it?"

"What if it does?"

"I'd say it's about time you came to your senses, young man, because it doesn't get any better!"

An hour or so later Karen arrived. We went for a walk and shared a lot of small talk. She asked me how school was going, and I asked her how work was going. We sat in the back yard, and I played and sang my song "What a Lucky Man Am I" for her. When I saw tears in her eyes I wasn't sure if she liked it that much or if it sounded that bad. Since she asked me to do it again for Bud and Phyl, I guess she liked it.

Karen and I spent most of our waking hours together during that spring break. The day I was due to leave, I met her in the parking lot behind the Ward store. We hugged and kissed and I asked her if she would like it if I drove down on the weekends to see her. She said she would love that. I think we both knew at that moment that we had met our soul mates. There by the grace of God and my Guardian Angel stood I.

When I returned to school, my roommates drilled me to find out what was going on. Who was this girl that I had fallen for? I showed them a graduation picture Karen had given me. I can still see Gust's jaw dropping to the floor when he looked at her picture and said, "How did you get so lucky, Saumer?"

Spring quarter was pretty much a waste of time as far as school was concerned. I was a love sick puppy. I was driving to Albert Lea every chance I got. I would skip classes to get an early start. Lab partners would try to cover for me, but I would end up failing exams. When all was said and done, our love for each other grew but I ended up failing two classes required for my Biology degree. I did manage to write a number of songs. The most important one being:

Come with me to a distant sea.
Let us walk hand in hand, sharing our love whenever we can.
Let us not take offense at one another's silence.
And let us gaze into the fire light, opening our minds to its
    colors so bright.

Oh come with me to a distant sea.
And if God be willing, then let that sea be one of love and
    tranquility.

So come with me to our distant sea.
And we will be free.
And we will be free.

I decided not to go to summer school but to go to Albert Lea and work, so I could be with Karen and get to know her family. Her twin brothers, David and Darrel, were in high school; her sister, Sheila, was in college at the U of M. Her father, Harry Chance, was a lineman for Dairyland Power. Her mother, Betty Chance, was a painter for Streaters.

I stayed with my Aunt and Uncle in their basement. If we weren't working, Karen and I spent every waking hour together: drive in movies, picnics in the parks and fields, moonlight swims, and walks around the lakes. There were days I would go to work on only a couple of hours of sleep.

Harry had gotten me a job with a road construction crew for the summer. But instead of working the road crew, they put me with a guy named Russ installing drain tile for drainage ditches. It was a great job. One day Russ and I were working with another man and his young son who were running a dragline. We needed to get a tractor from another field across the road. The man asked me if I knew how to drive a tractor. I told him I could. He sent me and his twelve or thirteen year old son to get the tractor. When we got to the tractor, the son insisted he should drive the tractor. "After all, it is my dad's!" I didn't care and I figured he knew what he was doing so I let him drive, and I stood on the tongue of the tractor.

All was going fine, until we got to the approach. The boy started to turn too sharp and was catching the corner of the ditch. I could feel the tractor starting to tilt to its side. As I jumped off the back end of the tractor, I reached over the seat and grabbed the boy by the collar of his shirt and pulled him up and over the back of the seat. We went rolling on the ground as the tractor went tumbling down the ditch.

The boy jumped up crying, "My glasses! My glasses! My dad will kill me. Where are my glasses?"

The boy had just had his life saved and a thousand dollar tractor lay at the bottom of the ditch, but he was worrying about his fifty dollar pair of glasses. I could relate to the boy's behavior and his fear of his father. We found his glasses all in one piece on the approach driveway. There by the grace of God and my Guardian Angel stood I and that boy.

As summer came to an end, Karen decided to move up to St. Cloud and find work. She didn't want me to fail anymore classes. She found a job with Web Publishing for a couple of months and then landed a wonderful job working at a day activity center for adult special needs people. Karen was so good working with the staff and students that she was offered the directorship, but certification problems kept that from happening. I was proud of her all the same.

Things worked out quite well for us while I was finishing school. Karen lived in a basement apartment with some other girls whom we hardly ever saw. We saw each other as often as possible. Our lives basically revolved around each other's. Classes got easier for me and I was writing songs constantly. Life was as good as it gets! The only dark time occurred while I was student teaching at Apollo High School in St. Cloud. I lost two very important people in my life. Uncle Bud died of a stroke and brother-in-Law, Donny, died of a heart attack.

One Friday in January, 1973, Karen and I were going to drive her little Pinto to Grand Forks, ND to see Robyn and Larry to celebrate Robyn's and my birthdays, which are only three days apart. Larry was stationed there at the Air Force Base. As we were pulling out onto the freeway, I had to stop while I was trying to merge with traffic. BOOM! Something hit us from behind. As we were getting out of the car, Karen was crying and shouting at the man who hit us, "What have you done to my car, my beautiful Studly?!" (Studly was her nickname for her Pinto)

We had been rear-ended by a Lincoln Continental. What followed was nothing short of a fairy tale. The man said he was deeply sorry and that he didn't want any trouble. Karen was crying about how he had ruined our trip to Grand Forks. He said he was an Urologist doctor and on his way to the hospital to perform surgery on a kidney patient. He didn't have time to involve the police. He asked us to follow him to the Ford dealership and he would line us up with a car for our trip and see to it that our damaged car was taken care of.

After about fifteen minutes at the Ford dealership, the manager came out and said the strangest thing, "Dr. Harburough would like you to come with me to our warehouse and pick out a car."

"What do you mean, pick out a car?" Karen asked.

"He wants to buy you a new car so you can get on your way to Grand Forks."

"You mean he is going to buy me a new car?"

"Yes, in exchange for your damaged Pinto."

"Doesn't this seem a bit strange to you?" Karen asked the manager.

"He'll pay cash for whatever car you pick, so I'm fine with it. All I need from you is your title."

"I'll have to call my dad for that."

After he made Karen repeat the story a half dozen times, Harry was on his way with the title. Meanwhile, Karen and I accompanied the manager to the warehouse to pick out her new car. It was love at first sight for Karen as she fixed her eyes on a metallic blue Pinto Hatchback. The manager said there would be no problem.

When Harry and Betty finally arrived, they couldn't believe their eyes when they saw Karen's beautiful new car. All the paper work was handled and Karen's folks saw us off. There by the grace of God and our Guardian Angel, Karen and I drove away in a brand new car.

I must confess, I never really proposed to Karen. We simply agreed one day that we were meant to be husband and wife. Karen didn't want an engagement ring, but asked that we buy a sewing machine instead so she could make her wedding dress. Once the decision to get married was made, Karen went to work planning the wedding of her dreams for May 26th, 1973. Our wedding was beautiful in every sense. It was held in a huge city flower garden along the Mississippi River in St. Cloud, on a beautiful Saturday morning. Lee and Gust stood up for me. Robyn and Sheila stood up for Karen. Aunt Phyl stood in for my mom with Dad. Harry and Betty walked Karen down a stone sidewalk while I sang a song I wrote, "Come With Me". About a hundred of our friends and family members were in attendance. The service was officiated by Karen's youth pastor, Papa John. The reception was at the park pavilion with all the food prepared by Karen and her mother.

The months of May and June flew by. With all the wedding preparations unfolding in May, we also managed to move into one of the Michigan Avenue apartments. After the wedding, we spent the next four days at a peaceful lake cottage, owned by some friends, in Brainerd, MN. They also left us some wine and steaks to help us celebrate. It was a simple but great honeymoon. I had to be back for a final exam on Wednesday and graduation was Saturday.

The summer was almost as hectic. I painted apartments to pay for our rent. I sent over a hundred job applications for teaching positions. One week, we went on a job interview trip to West Point, NE; Frost, MN; and River Falls, WI. I was offered positions at all three school systems. River Falls won hands down. I remember the day principal, DeWayne Meyer, from the River Falls Junior High School, called. Karen came running into the apartment I was painting, about a block away from ours, and told me to hurry because she thought it was the Principal at River Falls on the phone. When I answered the phone I heard, "Sempher Fi, Marine." I knew I had the job. I was to teach three classes of High School Biology and three classes of Junior High Life Science. I was also hired to coach freshmen football and junior high wrestling.

Karen and I drove to River Falls in July to look for a place to live because football practice started in mid-August. We got real lucky. There was a beautiful house for rent just one block away from the high school. We talked to the owner and she agreed to rent to us and agreed to let us do some painting and cleaning of the carpet and woodwork to get rid of the smell of cigar smoke. We spent two weekends running to River Falls to work on our home. We had it looking and smelling like new. One Sunday, Karen's cousins joined us at the house and were helping clean, when all of a sudden, the owner came barreling into the house yelling for everyone to get out. "I didn't agree to have a bunch of people I don't even know working on my house!" Karen and I were embarrassed and very hurt.

Our trip back to St. Cloud was quiet for a long time until Karen broke into tears and said she didn't think she wanted to rent from a lady who was so unappreciative of what we had done with the house. I was thinking the same thing, so we agreed to go back in the middle of the week and try to find something else.

Before we could go looking for an apartment, we needed to get some money for a deposit. We went to the River Falls State Bank to see about a loan on my first teacher's check. As it turned out, the president of the bank was on the school board and remembered the night the board approved my hiring. We told him about our ordeal with the house and lady. He knew who the lady was and assured us that she didn't represent River Falls. When his secretary brought the loan papers into his office, she told us she had an apartment that would be available for rent at the first of the month. If we wanted to look at it, we could go see it across from Glen Park. Her son and his family lived next door in the duplex. After finishing our business at the bank, we went to look at the duplex apartment. We couldn't believe it. It was everything we needed. The man who was living there agreed to let us take a closer look and also agreed to let us store things in the basement if we needed, which we did. We went back to the bank and told Jane Patricka that we would like to rent her apartment. Instead of a deposit, she asked me if I would mind doing some painting in the apartment.

We slowly drove to the house we had put so much time and effort into. What would we say to the "Bitch Lady" when we met her? Well, she made it easy for us. As we pulled into the driveway, she came out the front door. "Oh, I'm so glad to see you kids! I've been trying to call you to tell you that I've decided to rent the house to someone else. I think this house is just too much for you kids!"

Karen and I looked at each other in disbelief. How could this day be happening? It was like something or someone was controlling everything for us. We agreed with the "Bitch Lady". We got all our stuff we had been storing in the garage and stuffed it into the pinto. As we were getting ready to drive away, the lady came running up to the car and handed Karen a piece of paper and said, "I want to give you kids a little something for all the work you did on the house."

As we drove off, I looked over at Karen and saw her flooded in tears. "What's wrong?" I asked.

"She gave us a check for ten dollars!"

There by the grace of God and our Guardian Angel, drove Karen and me.

Chapter Fifteen

A SECOND GUARDIAN ANGEL

*O*ur little duplex apartment in the park turned out to be an even bigger blessing than we imagined. We were allowed to have pets so Karen was able to bring her cat, Duster, from St. Cloud. Karen bought a beautiful Golden Retriever puppy for my birthday in 1974. We named her Shammer. I was able to run and train her in the huge park field across the street. In future years she proved to be a fantastic hunting dog. Shammer did her best to convince us of that fact in her puppy years when she would bring anything you left on the floor out to the back yard to show the neighbors. She was especially fond of Karen's bras and panties.

Karen secured a job at Freeman's Drug store and developed a friendship with another worker there named, Starla Deiss. Starla and her husband, Gordy, have remained dear friends. We have many fond memories of times spent with the Deiss's, dancing, horseback riding, fishing, and partying.

Teaching turned out to be quite a challenge for my first year. I was split teaching three classes of tenth grade Biology at the high school in the morning and then traveling across town during my lunch time to teach two classes of junior high school Life Science and one class of

Earth Science. I spent a couple hours at home every evening prepping for the next day. Coaching ninth grade football was even more stressful. I coached with someone who had never coached before so we made a lot of mistakes. The biggest mistake of my coaching career happened on a road trip to Mondovi, WI. While we were on our way to Mondovi, Ray and I were busy planning for the game, and the bus driver failed to notice a detour sign. The next thing we knew we were in Menomonie, which wasn't on the way to Mondovi. Ray quickly told the bus driver to turn around because he missed the turn. When we finally got to the Mondovi high school athletic field, it was so late people were getting in their cars and going home. The game had been forfeited.

We started our return trip to River Falls. It wasn't long before some of the players started acting up. One of our many mistakes for the day was letting the cheerleaders travel on the team bus. A couple of the ballplayers started making sexual remarks toward one of the cheerleaders. Ray stood up and made a bold announcement, "If you don't clean up the language, Mr. Saumer and me are going to come around and tape your mouth so you can't say anymore!" Well, needless to say things didn't get any better. Ray handed me a bunch of tape and told me to go to the back of the bus and tape mouths, working my way back to the front. I was the assistant, so I did what I was told. After I had taped half a dozen mouths, I looked up only to see Ray sitting down. I quit taping and went and sat down also.

"What's going on here, Ray?"

"I don't think we should have taped their mouths," Ray answered.

"Then you shouldn't have made the threat. And why didn't you say something before I taped half a dozen players?"

The next day, the athletic director called for a special team meeting with himself and the Junior High Principal. He told us the phone rang off the hook the night before with questions from parents as to what had happened on the team bus. Principal Meyer asked for some players to tell their story as to what had happened. A couple of well mannered players spoke up and told the story just as it happened. Mr. Wunrow made the comment that a couple of players getting their mouth taped had been unfortunate, but they probably got off a lot easier than they would have if he had been their coach. Mr. Meyer dismissed the meeting with this advice to the players, "let the coaches do the coaching and you do the playing." The rest of the season went just fine. Some of the players on that team are very good friends of mine today—even one who got taped.

On our way back from the state wrestling tournament in February of 1974, I got an impulse to turn into the Wausau Home dealer in Hudson, WI, just to have a look at what they had to offer. We had been talking a little about buying a home so I thought it would be a good way to start investigating. We liked what we saw and their prices were right for us, they could line us up with special financing with FHA, and they even had a lot for us in River Falls. We made a deal for a home contingent on financing and an acceptable lot.

A week of so later, we got word that our financing had been approved. We weren't real keen on the lot locations they had to offer, but we did pick out one lot by the University football field. One day I mentioned to one of my seventh grade classes that we were looking for some land to put a house on. One of my students came up to me after class and said, "I think my dad is thinking about selling a chunk of our property. Would you like me to ask him to give you a call if he is?"

"Where is your property located?" I asked the young girl.

"We're just a little ways out of town. We have a really big yard. Dad has to mow it with a big tractor."

"That sounds really great, Lisa. Please ask your dad for me and have him give me a call." I handed her a piece of paper with my name and phone number on it. I couldn't wait to get home and tell Karen the potential good news.

By the time I got home, the surprise was on me. Karen was waiting for me with house plans and directions to the country lot. Lisa's father had already called and he invited us to meet him and look at the property as soon as I got home. We left without hesitation.

What a blessing! The property was two acres of well kept lawn with tall poplar trees across the front. Roamy and Lavone Thom walked us around the property and visited with us like they were our parents. They had another daughter the same age as Karen and married. Roamy had been a POW in WWII in Germany and had been a commercial painter for over twenty years. He was in his mid-fifties and the yard work was getting to be too much. They also had a lake home by Cumberland, WI, and wanted to be able to spend more time there as they were getting ready to retire when Lisa graduated.

We settled on a deal that same evening. The next day, I presented the option to the Wausau Home Dealer and they approved it. We were on our way to being country home owners. We moved into that home in the fall of '74. On August 30th of 1975, our first son, Brandon Jack was born. The rascal came out blue but regained his color quickly. What a joy he was! Karen always claimed he was the perfect baby, but she may have been a bit partial.

That same fall of '75, the two grandpas spent some good quality time together planting trees all day while I was teaching and coaching. What a treat it was to come home and see so much work accomplished. Herb and Harry made quite a tandem, dad in his mid sixties and Harry in his early fifties. Most of those trees are thirty feet tall today.

In the winter of 1977, Karen was pregnant again and Brandon was getting to be a bit of a hand full at about 17 or 18 months of age. Grandpa Herb came and stayed a week or so to help out by watching Brandon while Karen got some much needed rest. One early morning, Grandpa Herb woke up just in time to catch Brandon heading out the front door. We put hook locks on all the doors that day.

≈

Stacia LaRae Saumer was born on March 19th, 1977. She was the most beautiful thing on the face of the planet. Stacia always smiled. She looked you right in your eyes and grabbed your heart. Karen and I were in seventh heaven with the addition of a new baby girl to complete the "All American Dream Family": A good job, a new home, a new car (we had just bought a new Aspen Station Wagon), a family dog, a family cat, a baby boy, and now a new baby girl.

Just as December 7th, 1941 is the "Day of Infamy" for the United States, June 6th, 1977 is the "Day of Infamy" for the Saumer family. It had been the last day of the school year. I had run into town to pick up a tiller I was renting for the garden. As I pulled into the driveway, I saw Karen and LaVone standing together down by the garden with Brandon. I stopped inside the house for a drink. There, sound asleep in her swing-o-matic, was Stacia. I tucked her in, cranked up the swing some more, and went outside to join Karen and LaVone.

I told Karen that I had checked on Stacia and that she was fine. The three of us discussed the lay-out for the garden. After what seemed like fifteen minutes, we went up to the house to check on the baby. We opened the garage door to the house and walked in on every parent's worst nightmare. Stacia was dangling from the swing with the waist strap caught under her chin. She had managed to get both of her legs on one side of the crotch strap and started sliding down out of the swing but caught her neck on the strap.

All hell broke loose. I ran and got Stacia out of the swing and laid her on the floor to check her over. She was unconscious and wasn't breathing. LaVone ran and got Roamy and Lisa. Karen called for an ambulance. We worked frantically to get our precious princess to wake up and start breathing. Before I knew it, the paramedics rushed through the door, grabbed Stacia and out the door they went.

We followed the ambulance to the River Falls hospital. Lisa stayed back to watch Brandon. When we went inside the hospital, we were told they had already sent Stacia to Regions Hospital in St. Paul. We jumped back into the car and drove to St. Paul. All this time, Karen was sobbing and praying out loud that her precious baby girl would be all right.

We sat with Stacia through the night. She was hooked up to a respirator and had all kinds of cords attached to her head and body. She looked so helpless, so pure, and so innocent. We were told she had very little brain activity, and that she wasn't going to make it. That morning, I watched Stacia pass away in her mother's arms, as her mother sang "You are so beautiful to me". Our beautiful little world didn't seem so beautiful anymore. Why had God and my Guardian Angel allowed this to happen?

The loss of a family member is tough, but people somewhere are going through it every day. Some become stronger from it and some become weaker. Thanks to a strong support group, we became stronger. Karen's parents flew from Seattle, where they had been visiting Betty's brother. Grandpa Herb drove over with several other members of the family. When Dad came through the door of our home, he and I hugged one another like we had never done before. It was a little easier to imagine what Dad had gone through on January 27th, 1949. Aunt Phyl drove up from Albert Lea.

We had a very small funeral service at the Greenwood Cemetery with Pastor Mark Gartner officiating and choir director, Violet Bohn, singing "He". Grandpa Herb, in his quest to make up for the father figure he had seldom been, bought the grave marker headstone with the inscription "Our Little Lamb". Cards and flowers from teachers and friends from church flooded the home. Everything meant a great deal to both Karen and me.

After a week, when things had settled down a bit, we decided we would get away by driving Grandpa and Grandma Chance back to Seattle to get their car. We had bought a brand new Aspen Wagon about a month earlier so we had plenty of room and the wheels for the trip. It was our first trip across country with Betty and Harry. All was going fine until we got to Bozeman, Montana. As we were approaching the Bozeman exit, the car started jerking and the check engine light came on. We managed to get off the interstate and pulled in to the first service station we came to. They told us the Dodge dealership was around the corner and down three blocks. We cautiously drove our car to the Dodge dealer. Their service manager told us that the transmission had gone and they could have one flown in by the next day. We could be on our way by the following day. The car was under warranty and wouldn't cost us anything. However, we did have to get a room for two nights.

After we got checked into a room, Harry kept ragging on me to do this and to do that. I finally blew a gasket. I remember throwing something at the wall of the motel room and leaving.

When I returned to the room, I called the River Falls Dodge dealer I bought the car from and told him about my predicament. He was aware of our personal tragedy also. All our expenses ended up being covered for us which relieved a lot of stress.

The rest of the trip went well. We had a very nice visit with Karen's Aunt and Uncle in Seattle. We got to walk the beach with them and collect drift wood for her uncle's hobby. We spent a lot of time with Brandon. He loved the beach and ocean. As peaceful as everything seemed, we couldn't get over the fact that, a couple of weeks ago we also had a little girl. She would never get to see the ocean or walk the beach.

We honor Stacia's memory every year at Christmas when we put out a stocking on the mantel for each of our four children. Karen gives me an angel ornament for the tree every year. Stacia is our family's special Guardian Angel. Nevertheless, for the rest of us, life went on.

Chapter Sixteen
MY THREE SONS

"Life will go on and if we obey, there will be another moment, there'll be another day." I wrote that line in a song the summer Karen and I were dating in Albert Lea. I guess I never really recognized it for its importance. It is actually a statement of my philosophy of life. It's partly what this book is all about. We all experience good times and bad times in our life. But God promises us that He will never allow us to suffer more that we can bear. Life goes on all around us. God gave us the freedom to choose how we proceed with our life. If we obey his commission to love one another as Christ loved us, then there will be more days in our life filled with good times and bad.

A couple months after Stacia's death, Brandon turned two. A year later, God blessed us with another son, Shane. Two years after Shane, God blessed us with Travis. Our three sons became the focus of our life. We went to hundreds of football games, wrestling matches, and baseball games over the years. We loved it and miss it. The boys left us with many memories of their childhoods. I think each of them may have gotten a little help from a Guardian Angel a time or two.

≈

Brandon Jack Saumer needed help coming into the world on August 30th, 1975. He got hung up in delivery with the umbilical cord wrapped around his neck. When he finally came out, he looked like a big grape. The nurses rushed him off and got the fluids out of his lungs. In a matter of a few minutes he was fine and in his mother's arms. I had never experienced such a roller coaster ride of emotions from tension, to joy, to fear, and back to joy.

During his infancy, Brandon needed to wear a brace between his feet to help straighten out his legs so he wouldn't be pigeon-toed. The bar was handy to grab hold of and lift his legs up while you changed his diaper. When he started to walk, he needed special shoes. Eventually, he got straightened out. He went on to be a pretty good athlete in high school.

When he was in middle school, Brandon had dizzy spells and even passed out a couple of times. When doctors checked him over, they came to a conclusion that he was growing too fast and we had to feed him more. He's never quit eating; I think he still has that problem. Mom was happy because his history of passing out kept him out of the military.

My most memorable moment with Brandon is when we were fishing in Canada and he netted a seven and a half pound Walleye for me.

Brandon is now in his thirties. He has a wonderful job as the maintenance supervisor for a retirement and long term care facility in River Falls. Tenants are always telling me about how thoughtful and caring he is. Brandon has been recognized by his friends for his love and devotion by including him in over a dozen wedding parties. I kid him with "always a groomsman but never the groom". He always says, "In due time." I'm not sure what he means by that.

≈

On June 3rd, 1978 God blessed us with Shane Robert Saumer. I'm sure Shane could write a book of his own life experiences that would equal or exceed this one. After one of Shane's little escapades, I phoned

Dad to tell him about it. His only comment was, "I guess the acorn didn't fall too far from the tree, did it?"

When he was an infant, Shane needed a little guardian angel help. One day, while I was changing his diaper, I noticed Shane's ribs were sticking out quite a bit. He looked like he had lost a lot of weight. After several weeks of medical exams, it was decided he had a problem called Celiac Disease. The villa in his small intestines was not developing so he couldn't digest protein. We had to feed him rice cereal and banana for several months. He grew out of the condition but still has a pretty sensitive digestive system.

Shane was always a dare devil in his youth. I'm sure I don't know all the things he did as a child, just like my father didn't know all the things I did. I'm very aware of one stunt because he broke his arm doing it. He hung from the swinging walk bridge at Glen Park when he was about eight. Upon scaling the guide rope to the bridge, he let go and fell to the ground about twenty feet below. Another two feet over and it would have been a fall to his death about one hundred feet or more to the bottom of the ravine. He was lucky to survive with only a broken arm.

My most memorable moment with Shane is our fly-fishing trip to Yellowstone National Park in Montana. We camped out of our Dodge Caravan and fished several different rivers. Shane was in his glory; I don't know if I have ever seen him as happy and at peace.

Shane now has a family of his own—his wife Bethany; her son, Jonathan; his daughter, Brooklyn; their daughter, Holly; and their son, Chance. Shane makes me proud when I see the love he has for his family, friends, and nature.

≈

Travis Chance Saumer blessed us with his arrival into the world on October 23rd, 1980. He scared the heck out of us when his heart stopped beating while in the monitoring room at Region's Hospital in

St. Paul. Karen was giving birth at Region's because she was a month overdue as a result of a broken leg she had suffered eight months into her pregnancy. Mom and Dad were a little shook up, but Travis survived the ordeal just fine.

It seemed like Travis was "an accident looking to happen" growing up. He had to have had a guardian angel looking after him. He had five sets of stitches in one year. Although we laughed about it and called him "Stitch Saumer", we were afraid that Social Service was going to come knocking at our door to haul us away for neglect.

Travis also grew to be a very good athlete in high school. Baseball was his passion. When he was fifteen, I took him on a stadium tour attending Major League games on the way to Boston where we watched the Red Sox play the Twins. We went to Cooper's Town Baseball Hall of Fame. We slept in the Caravan most of the time. During his senior year in Legion Baseball, he played in the State All Star game where he hit a ground rule double and scored twice.

Travis has grown to be quite a young man with a family of his own—his wife, Cathy and son, Alex, (plus one on the way). I am proud to see the man he has become.

My most memorable moment, with the three boys all together, is our family vacation to the Black Hills of South Dakota. I am grateful that the three boys have remained close to each other. They have played softball together, golfed together, fished together, stood up for one another in weddings, and now they get together on special occasions so their kids can play with each other.

Chapter Seventeen

LIFE SUPPORT

*T*hroughout my life, God has provided me with a tremendous support network of family and friends. While I was growing up, I had my father, brother and sisters, aunt and uncle, grandma and grandpa, and my friends and some of their parents. My best friends through high school were Mike Jacob and his brother Craig. I'm sure their parents, Don and Helen, felt like they had adopted another son. They always made me feel welcome and treated me with respect. They had a big impact on my life as a model of good parenting. Whenever we are in Montevideo, I do my best to stop at the Jacob house for a visit and a cup of coffee.

College created a whole new set of friends. I have found that adult friendships are generally long lasting and sometimes life-lasting. Although your friendship may be interrupted due to time or space, the bond you created in college is strong enough to bring you back together when the opportunity presents itself. It has been thirty-six years since our college graduation. My college friends and their spouses: Lee and Peggy, Gust and Jonelle, Rod and Jean, Billy and Suzanne, and Mudd and Linda get together with us on various occasions each year to rekindle our friendships.

While teaching and living in River Falls, God has provided me with unbelievable support groups. Teachers, in general, are a close-knit group. They would rise to almost any occasion in support of each other. I'll never forget the love and support we got from Dave and Jane Amdahl at the hospital when Stacia died. I will never forget the day in late October when we built our second home. Someone let the word out that I was going to side my house on a day off from teaching. Several teachers showed up to help side in the falling snow. Principal, DeWayne Meyer saw me through some pretty tight situations over the years. My greatest support group from teaching came from the Seven Blue Team at Meyer Middle School. Although the team members changed over the years, we were always there for each other: Ron, Gail, Tom, Carole, Todd, John, Deb, Kris, and Rita. Each has a special quality and I thank God for putting them in my life.

Members of Luther Memorial Church have also been a strong support in my life. They have helped us get through troubled times and helped us raise our three boys. I'll always remember the night when about twenty members from church arrived to help insulate the house we were building. (Pastor Herb had a lot to do with that). A church marriage encounter at St. Thomas resulted in a support group with five other couples from Luther Memorial. We have become dear friends over the years: Brian and Ellen, Mark and Sandi, Bob and Jean, Al and Jan, and Herb and Carol. For over twenty years, we have been getting together every two months to do something special. We have watched each other's children grow. We appreciate each other's strong Christian faith.

Of course Karen's parents and family provided support throughout the years. They have all become more than in-laws; they have become dear friends. I lost one of my best friends when Harry died in 2004. Betty has become the mother I never had and a very dear friend. Sheila's time share vacations to Washington D.C. and Hawaii are very memorable.

≈

The Lord has blessed us with lake property near Amery, Wisconsin, where we can have special moments with family and friends. The story about the acquisition of the property is quite bazaar and yet inspirational. Here is how it played out:

"Hey, Dad, why are you going this way to Wapi?" Shane asked, as we were on our way to go fishing one hot August day in 1996.

"I don't know. I just thought it would be nice to see some different scenery. We can stop in Star Prairie for bait. "

After getting bait, we resumed our trip to Lake Wapogasset about two miles west of Amery, Wisconsin. It was a cloud covered day and my hopes were high on catching some nice Walleyes. We were tooling down county road "C" when Shane said, "Look at that sign! It says 'Lake Lots for Sale'. I never knew there was a lake back there."

"Neither did I. Let's check it out on the way back home."

We spent about four hours fishing Wapi and having a great time without catching a keeper.

"Why don't we go check out that little lake where the sign was?" I suggested.

"Sounds good to me," replied Shane. "I would like to find another good fishing lake. Wapi seems to be dying out."

We loaded up the boat and headed down county road "C" to where we had seen the sign. The winding road took us back to a small beautiful lake with only a few homes on it. We slowly drove along looking for empty lots with for sale signs. We saw some empty lots but no signs. Finally, at the bottom of a small hill on what looked like a couple of huge lots, was a man standing by a pontoon boat. I stopped the car and rolled down the window and yelled. "Excuse me sir. Are these the lots that are for sale?"

"No! But they could be!" The man yelled back as he started walking up to our car.

"Hi. My name is Lanny and this is my son Shane. We saw the sign at the entrance saying 'Lake Lots for Sale' so we thought we would check it out."

"Oh, that old sign has been there for years. I think it's for some lots down the road," the man replied as he finished walking up to the car. "I'm David Mathews. These two lots are mine and I live right over there." He pointed to a beautiful home across the cul-de-sac. "Would you like to take a look at the property?"

"Yes we would."

The man gave us a complete tour of the two lots. I was in awe as I looked out onto the lake from the wooded point of the property; the view was breath-taking.

"What kind of fish do you catch in this lake?" Shane asked David.

"Pan fish, bass, and northern," David answered.

"I can't get over how clear the water is for this time of the year," I commented.

"King Lake is spring fed with no inlet or outlet," David replied.

I asked David what he wanted for the two lots. He gave me a quote for each separate lot and the two lots together. He told me about himself and his wife. He was a disabled Vietnam Marine Vet and she was disabled from a car accident. He gave me his name and phone number. I told him I was a Vietnam Marine Vet also. We thanked him for the tour and information.

As we were driving away, Shane commented, "Those sure were a couple of nice lots on a beautiful, small, peaceful lake."

I don't think I even replied. My mind was racing a hundred miles an hour. It had always been my dream to retire on a lake someday. How could I ever afford to purchase something like this? I thought about it all the way home. I told Shane not to say anything to Mom about the lake property. That night, I lay awake in bed most of the night thinking about the lake property and asking God for guidance. I decided to put it all in his hands; "His will be done".

It was Thursday, and it was Karen's day off from work. I asked her if she would like to go to Turtle Lake Casino for supper. Of course she said, "Yes, I'd really like that." So off we went.

"Why are we going this way to Turtle Lake?" Karen asked.

"I thought we would take in some different scenery," I replied.

"Why are you turning here?" Karen asked, as I turned at the sign saying "Lake Lots for Sale".

"There is something I want you to see."

"Oh honey, look at this beautiful little lake tucked back in here," Karen said. "Are you looking at property on this lake?"

"Don't get too excited; we're just looking!"

We toured the lots and walked down to the point. It took our breaths away and Karen fell in love.

We spent the month of September checking out lake property for sale in Western Wisconsin. Each time we would go and look at something we would stop back at King Lake. Nothing compared in beauty or price. How could we ever make this work? I concluded: If it was His will, The Lord would provide a way.

I called Dave and Jean Matthews and asked them if they would consider selling the lot with the point on a contract for deed. I think my heart stopped for a moment when they called back and said yes.

The next day, I went to my banker and laid out the situation and asked if I could get a loan for the down payment for the property. He said yes!

I went to my lawyer to review the abstract for the property. He suggested I present an offer to the Matthews for both the lots for a lower price, at a slightly higher interest, with a slightly higher down payment. We did as he suggested.

Thanks to our Lord, on October 16th, 1996 we signed a contract with the Matthews and became the owners of two beautiful acres of lake property. Karen is now Queen of King Lake.

I will never forget the rainy day in late October when we went to Northern Minnesota to bring Betty's and Harry's camper trailer to Amery to put on our King Lake lots. Harry, Betty, Karen, and I were to meet a friend, Pete Linn, from River Falls at Elm Island Lake, near Aitkin, Minnesota. Pete had agreed to pull the camper with his pickup truck.

Everything started out pretty good. We got the trailer hooked up with all the lights working. However, as Pete started pulling the trailer, the tail end bottomed out in the soft soil. We worked endlessly in the pouring rain getting the trailer out of the mud. We had to jack up the back end of the trailer to get the back wheels out of the mud and then pull it forward with the truck. Betty and Karen watched as we performed the maneuver three times; we were finally free from the mud. I rode along with Pete; we pulled the trailer down Interstate Highway 35 and onto US Highway 8.

Crossing over the St. Croix River into Wisconsin at St. Croix Falls, Highway 8 has a very steep climb out from the valley. We could see the pickup's heat gauge rising as we climbed the hill. There was no way we could stop mid-way up the hill. The truck could never pull the trailer from a dead stop going up the steep hill. We kept climbing; the heat gauge kept climbing.

When we finally made it to the top of the hill, we pulled into a gas station. We waited about a half hour for the truck to cool down. Pete checked everything over; we were good to go. Off we went with Harry, Betty, and Karen following.

It was raining "cats and dogs" when we finally reached King Lake. Pete pulled the trailer in through some trees and onto the lot. We had already decided we would park the trailer down by the point and the camp site. Once again, the back end of the trailer dug into the soil as Pete reached the bottom of the hill. This time he just kept on going.

Once we had the trailer parked, we were too wet and too cold to do anything else. We decided we would wait until spring to level everything. We simply blocked the tires and we were on our way home. What a great friend Pete was!

Spring couldn't get here soon enough. We were all anxious to get up to the lake and get the trailer set up and start enjoying the lake. One week-end, Betty and Harry came up to help. Karen had to work so it was just the three of us.

Harry and I got the trailer leveled and secured. Things were looking pretty good so we decided to take the boat out and go fishing. Betty said, "I would rather dink around the camp site." So Harry and I set off fishing.

Karen was pulling into camp just as we were coming in from fishing. Betty was sitting in a lawn chair next to the fire pit with a beautiful fire blazing away.

"What a beautiful fire!" Karen exclaimed as she got out of her car.

"I suppose you've managed to pick up every stick in these woods while we were out fishing," Harry said to Betty as we approached the fire.

"No. I was busy building a new fire pit!" Betty snapped back.

We all looked at the fire pit. It was magnificent, with huge boulders around it. Some of them had to weigh a hundred pounds or more. "Where did you get those boulders and how did you move them?" asked Harry.

Betty just sat there with a grin on her face. She finally looked at me and said, "They were in the back of the trailer hidden behind the bed. They're from the fire pit we had at Elm Island."

"You mean they were in the trailer when we brought it here?" I asked. "That explains why the back end was bottoming out all the time."

"Betty, Betty, Betty!" Harry sighed. "You stood and watched as we dug that damn trailer out of the mud over and over again."

"Well, what's done is done!" I commented.

Karen chimed in with, "They make a beautiful fire pit!"

I can see how Betty rolled those boulders, one by one, out of the trailer and set them in place in the fire pit thirty feet from the trailer. I'm still puzzled as to how, at age 68 and only weighing 120 pounds, she lifted those boulders into the trailer by herself. But then again, she also had both of her knees replaced when she was 78. I guess she's just tough! We have enjoyed Betty's fire pit over the years and get a good laugh when someone retells its story.

I cherish the moments we spend at the lake each year with family and friends, as we get together on Memorial Day, 4th of July, and Labor Day. Here by the grace of God and my Guardian Angel stand me and my friends and family.

Chapter Eighteen
TROUBLED WATERS

*F*ishing has developed into one of my passions. For twelve years I went to Canada on a fishing trip with several friends. In 1996, we purchased the King Lake property by Amery, Wisconsin. Since we were paying for lake property, I couldn't justify spending money to go to Canada to go fishing so I quit going.

In May of 2000, we sold the house we were living in on South Ridge Road and began construction of the house we now live in on Foster Court. Construction was going pretty slow in June when a friend asked me to go with him and his wife to Chamberlain, SD and fish for walleyes. I knew I had a lot of work ahead of me for the summer, but I couldn't resist and said yes. Dave Frank and I ended up having a wonderful time and kindled a great friendship.

Jean Frank didn't like to fish and preferred staying home, so the next year David and I went to Chamberlain by ourselves. We should have gotten the message that it was going to be a tough trip when we ended up in the last room at Allen's Fishing Lodge. As I look back, I don't know if I would have let my dog stay in that room. The air conditioning didn't work, the beds sagged to the floor, and the bathroom was so small you couldn't turn around once you closed the door.

On our second day of fishing, we decided to go to Fort Thompson Dam to put in for the day. For the first half of the day, that turned out to be an excellent decision. After we put in, we went down stream to what is called the "Big Bend". By noon, we had four nice Walleyes in the boat and had thrown a dozen little ones back. We were having a fantastic outing.

A boat came rushing past, waving to us, and pointing toward the landing. A few minutes later, another boat came rushing by making the same motions. We figured there must be a hell of a storm coming, so everyone was heading in. We decided to join everyone else and started for the landing which was about a mile back up stream around the bend.

As we rounded the bend, we couldn't believe our eyes. The wakes were three and four feet high. The wind was gusting down the river. Tucked away behind the bend, we had been sheltered from the winds. David did his best to captain us against the wakes. The boat was taking quite a beating, as well as our backs and rear ends.

One of the boats that had rushed by us looked like it was stranded in a cove. As we made our way toward the man and boy, they waved us on letting us know they were okay. Dave continued the battle against the current, the rain, the wind, and the wakes like a valiant captain.

It was hopeless. We had to beach the boat. We thought we had gotten lucky when we saw a cove with a small stream empting into it. David made way toward shore and navigated us into the stream. We sat out the rest of the storm. When we were ready to leave, we discovered our troubles had only just begun.

Once the storm had settled, there wasn't as much water in the stream. Our boat had been lifted and set down on the bank time and time again. We were truly beached with only the motor and the back three feet of the boat in the water.

David jumped to the far side of the little stream. I threw him the bow guide rope. David pulled the bow as I tried to push. We could hardly budge the eighteen foot monster. I figured I could be more help if I joined David on the other bank and we both pulled on the rope. Rather than climb up into the boat and jump over to the other side like David had done, I decided to wade across the eight foot stream. On about my third step I was up to my crotch in mud and sinking fast. It was like what you see in the movies when someone steps into quick sand. The water was up to my chest, then my armpits, and then my shoulders.

I yelled at David, "Throw me the damn rope!"

He attempted to throw me the rope but he was stepping on part of it so it didn't make it to me.

"Throw it again!" I yelled.

When I got the rope, I was able to pull myself up to the bow of the boat, and then, walk out of the water and mud holding on to the side of the boat. I threw the rope back over to David, and then, went upstream and found a place to cross safely.

After several failed attempts to pull the bow of the boat into the water, I turned to David and said, "I think we're going to have to walk to the landing and get help."

"I don't think I can make it, Lanny," David said, as he stood shivering. We both knew that was the truth. David is asthmatic and has emphysema.

I decided I would go back over the hill to the cove where the other boat was stranded and ask them for help. All I could think about, as I walked to the other cove, was rattlesnakes in the grass. When I made it to the other cove, there was no sign of the other boat. They hadn't gone by us. I figured they must have gone back down stream to do some more fishing. Now what would we do?

As I was making my way back to David and the boat, I did a lot of talking and praying to God. "Lord, I know that if I am to see the light of another day, you will provide a way for us to get out of this mess."

No sooner had I told David that the other boat was no longer there, then we heard voices coming from around the bend. Suddenly two bodies appeared. It was the man and boy from the other boat. They were two coves over, not one. They had buried their prop in the mud and couldn't get out. They were walking back to the landing for help.

The four of us were able to get our boat back in the water. Then we took them back to their boat and the three of us, with David pulling with our boat, were able to get their boat free. However, their boat wouldn't run so we towed them to the landing.

At that point, cleaning fish was the last thing I wanted to do so we gave the man and his son the fish we had caught.

When we got back to the motel, we went to the adjoining restaurant for supper. It had just closed for the night. David did some sweet talking and the waitress and cook made us something to eat. What a day! There by the grace of God and my Guardian Angel sat David and I eating a most appreciated meal.

Two years later I bought that boat from David and he started parking his camper at our lake each summer.

So life has gone on and there have been many moments: college graduation for Karen as well as a couple of job changes, a master's degree for me, the building of two new homes, the purchase of lake property; the loss of Grandpa Herb, Aunt Phyl, cousins Blake, Brian, and Lorna, and Grandpa Harry Chance; and the life and death of three dogs and four cats. Our three sons have grown, graduated, and have started families of the own. And there will be many more moments and many more days. I'm sure our grandchildren will provide us with many memorable moments.

Chapter Nineteen
RECONCILIATION

*W*hen my father died in 1991, I asked my brother and sisters to let me give the eulogy at Dad's funeral service as a final act of reconciliation. The following is a copy of that eulogy:

DAD, POP, AND GRANDPA

Herbert Arthur Saumer was born in 1909, in Montevideo, Minnesota and was adopted into the Harry Saumer family in 1916. Pictures sent to Betty a couple of weeks ago, by dad's sister, Linnie, in Reno, Nevada, gave witness to what seemed to be a warm loving childhood. We had a lot of fun seeing dad as we had never seen him before. I could clearly see a close resemblance of dad in a picture of Kenny with his tongue sticking out.

Herb was an active youth while going to school in Montevideo. He was an excellent athlete and was elected captain of his football and track teams and played basketball. He graduated in 1928 from

Montevideo High School and went on to one year of college at St. 01af.

Herb married Ruth Gamm in 1933 and became the kingpin of 3 daughters and 2 sons, 19 grandchildren and 19 great-grandchildren. The name Herb became synonymous with "Dad", "Pop", and most often "Grandpa".

Hard times seemed to play a major role in dad's life; with mother's death in 1949; followed by many jobs at the Old Mill, Swift, and G.T.A.; and many homes. Despite the hard times, dad worked hard to fulfill a promise he had made mother to keep the family together.

As a father, a quote from Socrates has stuck in my mind ever since senior English class, "When I was a young boy my father knew very little, now that I am older, I'm amazed at how much he has learned." Dad was one of the founders of "tough love". He enforced strict rules and discipline; yet was caring, compassionate, and fun loving. I remember dad waiting at the door at 10:00 o'clock curfew, accepting no excuses for being 5 or 10 minutes late. I remember the same man ironing his daughter's dress and brushing her hair to get her ready for her first dance. He made us study our catechism lessons every Friday night and made us walk to confirmation class and Sunday school every week. But, confirmation day was always a big family celebration with lots of pictures, laughter, and plenty to eat. The effects of those times are still an important part of my life.

Dad was a great listener. The night before my high school graduation we talked about my childhood while he ironed my graduation gown. Afterwards, we hugged and forgave each other for all the grief we had caused one another.

My Guardian Angel

What greater love can a father give his children than the love he gives his grandchildren? Grandpa surely loved his grandchildren and his great-grandchildren. We all have precious moments of grandpa to remember: playing hide the thimble, playing softball at the Hermanson farm, pitching horseshoe, playing cards, and of course, watching the Vikings and the Twins, which he threatened to never watch again every time they lost. I know of a couple of grandchildren that would sneak down to visit with grandpa at work to get a nickel or a dime from him. Grandpa's door was always open if you needed to bend an ear, or to simply watch the ball game. And of course, there were always the Christmas envelopes from Grandpa.

Dad spent his retirement years living with Betty, the cornerstone of the family he created; whose love and care allowed him to take up many of the things he had given up in his life, such as: gardening, golf, fishing, and trips to visit each of us and our families.

82 years of loving, caring, and laughing is a good life.

Dad, rest easy in knowing that you have fulfilled your promise!

God bless you and keep you in his loving family in paradise!

In loving memory of Dad

Lanny

2/15/91

Chapter Twenty

A LIFETIME OF EDUCATION

*E*ducation has been a constant force in my life since I entered kindergarten at age five. I have either been going to school, teaching school, supporting someone going to school, or helping to build a school. The following is a timeline of education in my life:

1954 – 1967   Attended public school in Montevideo, Minnesota.

1967 – 1968   Attended St. Cloud State College.

1968 – 1969   Mentored squad members in USMC boot camp.
Attended CAP school in Vietnam
Helped build a school in Ahn Hi, Vietnam village

1969 – 1973   Attended St. Cloud State College and got a
BS degree in Biology

1973 - 2004   Taught science in the River Falls, Wisconsin public
school system
I got a Masters Degree from the University of
Wisconsin at River Falls
Karen got an AA degree in Interior Design from
Dakota County Tech. College

        I got an elementary education certification
        from UWRF
        Brandon attended two years of college at
        UW LaCrosse
        Shane attended one year at Chippewa Valley
        Technical College
        Travis attended one year of college at Winona
        State University

2005 – Present I supervise Student Teachers for the UWRF
        Raising funds for the building of an elementary
        school in Vietnam

Education has been my life because it saved my life. It is the direction my Lord and Guardian Angel have guided me. There is nothing in the world as awesome and empowering as learning. I will continue to supervise student teachers as long as I am able. I would like to say that there will be no end to my teaching. Upon my death, after all my healthy organs are donated for transplantation, my body will be donated to a Medical School for study.

Chapter Twenty-One
MY WAR

My personal war began in the fall of 2001. I was having trouble singing in the church choir. I would always start coughing in the middle of a song. I couldn't hold a note very long or sing a full line with one breath. Other than those little problems I felt fine and teaching had never been better.

It has become apparent to me that the Lord knew what was in store for me. I believe he inspired Karen to give me a gift certificate for piano lessons for Christmas in 2000. I started taking piano lessons with Lori Fuller in the spring of 2001. Lori was a wonderful piano teacher. She also was interested in my song writing. We spent some time working on writing the score to a couple of my songs. Lori suggested that I make a CD recording of my songs and referred me to a recording studio that she and her husband, Mike, who is one of the Meyer Middle School band instructors, were familiar with.

I struggled through the months of September and October of 2001 secretly recording a CD to give to Karen for Christmas. Every Thursday evening, while Karen was at work, I would go to the Brick House Recording Studio in River Falls and rush to get back home before her at 9:30 PM. We would record two songs each night, if my voice would last. We completed the CD in October. The recording technician at the studio referred me to a place in St. Paul where I could have multiple copies made. After giving the CD to Karen, I decided to give it to all of our friends and family as an expression of love and appreciation.

Everything seemed to center around my voice. I coughed when I sang. I coughed when I talked on the phone. I thought I might have a problem with my Larynx or voice box. In January 2002, I saw an Ear, Nose, and Throat specialist and found nothing wrong with my Larynx. They X-rayed my lungs and found nothing wrong. I went to an allergist and found nothing wrong. There wasn't any problem with teaching or my carpentry and home inspection businesses. I was becoming quite frustrated, but we just kept plodding along.

In May of 2003, I sang for my son, Shane's wedding. It was the worst performance of my life. I put my guitar in its case and didn't take it out for almost a year. In the spring of 2004 I sang for my students because I was retiring from teaching at the end of the school year. Singing for my students didn't seem to go too bad so I started playing and singing again. It wasn't long before I was having trouble again. I put my guitar away for good.

For two years, from the spring of 2004 to the spring of 2006, I poured myself into my work as a carpenter, home inspector, and a student teaching field supervisor for the UWRF. In March and April of 2006 I went to Vietnam with an organization called The D.O.V.E. Fund (The Development of Vietnam Endeavors). On that trip we took some walks and made some climbs that got me quite winded, like I had never been before.

Upon return from my trip, I resumed my normal work routine. However, I progressively got worse month by month. A chest X-ray in December of 2006 showed what my doctor said looked like fibrous infiltrates in my lungs. He referred me to a lung specialist, Dr. Wright, at the Minnesota Lung Center in Woodbury, MN.

THE LUNG CENTER BATTLE

After two months of testing, Dr. Wright's diagnosis was that I had Pulmonary Fibrosis, a progressive terminal scaring of the lung tissue. One type of fibrosis could be effectively treated and slowed down with steroids and the other type could not and was called Idiopathic Pulmonary Fibrosis (IPF). He told us the average life expectancy for people with IPF is about five years from the time of their diagnosis. It wasn't clear which type I had. We declared war on this disease and started a steroid treatment of Prednisone and prayed that it wasn't IPF.

As we drove down the interstate on our way home, I looked over at a sobbing wife. Karen looked at me and said, "What if it's IPF and you only have a few years to live? I don't know what I would do without you!"

"Let's not worry about that. Let's see if this steroid treatment works. If it does, I could have a lot of years left in me. If it doesn't I'll get a lung transplant and have even more years."

"Just don't you die on me or I'll kill you!" Karen declared, with a face full of tears.

We both let out a well needed laugh.

After a couple months of treatment, I complained to Dr. Wright about having some chest pain and sometimes I felt like I was going to jump out of my skin. There had been a few times where I had to pull off to the side of the road because of chest pain. I was told it was most likely the side affects of the Prednisone.

I struggled through the summer of work with a couple of incidents. I almost passed out in an attic during a home inspection. Building a deck required taking a break every hour to catch my breath and spend five minutes coughing and spitting up junk. We went to the Minnesota State Fair in August. We had to come home early because my blood-pressure went sky high. By October, I simply couldn't work anymore.

On November 8th, 2007, Dr. Wright concluded that because I wasn't responding to the steroid treatment, I most likely had IPF. Only with a full lung biopsy would we know for sure. He recommended we have one performed as soon as possible. We had lost our battle at the lung center.

THE MAYO BATTLE

With help from Dr. Wright, we were able to go to Mayo Clinic in early December for a two day evaluation and second opinion. We made an announcement to family and friends, via our Christmas news letter, informing them of my condition and asking them for their support through payer. God has blessed me with a wonderful support team. People are simply beautiful.

After an unbelievable series of tests, lung specialists at Mayo came to the same conclusion as Dr. Wright. I would need a full lung biopsy to make a final diagnosis. We had lost our battle at the Mayo.

THE VAMC BATTLE

Due to mounting expenses, on December 20th, I turned my care over to the VA Medical Center in Minneapolis, Minnesota. On January 14th, 2008 a lung biopsy revealed fibrosis due to chronic hypersensitivity pneumonia. Dr. Rubins, my pulmonologist, started a second treatment of Prednisone and night time oxygen.

We went to Hawaii for two weeks in March and April of 2008. The only thing I had any trouble with was snorkeling in rough ocean water; it simply took too much energy. But, we found some tide pools that were nice and calm and we snorkeled for hours; it was fantastic! I was able to golf a few times that summer with minor discomfort.

In August, I was experiencing some chest pain again. Dr. Rubins ordered a stress test to make sure my heart was okay. I passed the stress test so we resumed treatment. The chest pains became more frequent and stronger. Pulmonary Function Tests kept declining. In December, he made the call to start a lung transplant evaluation. Were we losing the battle at the VAMC?

The transplant evaluation involved a series of medical exams - physical, social, and mental. On February 6th, 2009, during one of those physical tests called a CT scan, it was discovered that I had a Pulmonary Emblus, or clot, in each of my Pulmonary Arteries. I spent the next four days in the VA hospital undergoing anti-coagulant treatment. On the fourth day, I was able to walk a mile for the first time in months without shortness of breath and no chest pain. My transplant evaluation was put on hold until my Warfarin therapy stabilized. We thanked the Lord for his blessing in disguise and for all the support from family and friends.

We resumed the transplant evaluation in early March. A Cardiac Ultrasound revealed that I had a mild case of congestive heart failure due to the Pulmonary Embli. It was felt that this should improve with time as the Warfarin works on the clots.

One of the final physical tests of the evaluation is an Angiogram which is actually a surgical procedure. To do this test meant I would have to go off my Warfarin treatment to lower the risk of bleeding during the surgery. During the procedure, on April 24th, it was discovered that I had three 90% blocked Coronary Arteries. My cardiologist said that if I didn't correct the situation I would surely have a heart attack. I was kept on the operating table and three stents were installed. Two days later I was on my way home thanking God for another blessing in disguise.

On May 5th, 2009 my lung transplant evaluation was completed and sent to Washington D.C. for review and placement on the VA national lung transplant list. On July 7th, we received word that my request was denied due to too many heart problems. On July 9th, my pulmonologist submitted a letter of appeal on my behalf. All that is left for me at this point is to continue my war against this disease through medical treatment and prayer and wait for "the phone call".

Acknowledgment

It is now July 23rd as I write this final chapter of My Guardian Angel. The writing of this book has been a major front in my war. It has opened my eyes to many of God's blessings throughout my life. It has strengthened the love I feel for my wonderful wife and best friend, Karen. It has strengthened my friendship with my former teaching colleague, Gail Andersen, who has been my first draft editor and confidante. I am grateful for the words of encouragement, "I want more stories" from my sister-in-law and second editor, Sheila Chance. I am also grateful to my pastor, Reverend Michael Scholz, for sharing his view with me that my book is a living testament to Psalm 91:9–16:

> "9 If you make the Most High your dwelling—
>   even the LORD, who is my refuge-
> 10 then no harm will befall you,
>   No disaster will come near your tent.
> 11 For he will command his angels concerning you
>   To guard you in all your ways;
> 12 they will lift you up in their hands,
>   so that you will not strike your foot against a stone.
> 13 You will tread upon the lion and the cobra;
>   You will trample the great lion and the serpent.

14 'Because he loves me,' says the LORD, 'I will rescue him;
    I will protect him, for he acknowledges my name.
15 He will call upon me, and I will answer him;
    I will be with him in trouble,
    I will deliver him and honor him.
16 With long life will I satisfy him
    and show him my salvation.'"
    (BibleGateway.com—NIV—1984)

Whether or not my mother has been my Guardian Angel throughout my life is questionable, but it makes me feel good to think that she has. It has given me a bond with her that I never got to have as a child. God has given me a free will, but I believe that ultimately it is God who controls everything. I am only here to give witness to his love, grace, and mercy. I love the lyrics in a song by Kurt Johnson, "Let the glory go to God alone. For we are but the instruments in our master's perfect plan, merely tools in the Potter's hands."

FAMILY

1972 Betty Carol Jill Ken Dad Lanny

2002 Ken Carol Lanny Betty Jill

Shane-Lanny-Brandon-Karen-Travis

Karen-Darrel-Betty-Sheila-David-Harry

Grandchildren

FRIENDS

Church

Wises Kovatchs Schultzs Saumers Sickberts Hoefers

College

Carlsons Holmvig -Johnsons Schmitzs Saumers

Teaching

Nelson - Vogler – Saumer - Rasmussen - Mottaz - Andersen - Witt - Meyer

Dave & Jean Frank

Lanny   Lee   Gust

Donny & Helen Jacobs

Bob & Marylou Tilt